The doomsday numbers had counted down to zero

When Mack Bolan was satisfied that there was no one left alive in the brothel, he got down to business, pitched one thermite bomb upstairs and dropped another in the small administrative office. He tossed a third grenade behind the bar and sprayed the ranks of liquor bottles with his Uzi, adding fuel to help the coming flames take hold.

Outside, pedestrians were staring, drawn by the sounds of gunfire and the rapid exodus of working girls, but Bolan made no effort to conceal his face.

Nobody tried to stop Bolan, and no one followed him as he walked the long block to his rental car. The fire was something tangible, and women—many of them almost nude—were spilling from adjacent houses now, as fire alarms began to clamor on the street. It was enough of a diversion that the Executioner could slip away, if not unnoticed, then at least forgotten in the crush.

Thus far, he had been concentrating on the local Triad and ignoring its political connection with Beijing. But all of that was about to change. The Executioner was seeing Red.

MACK BOLAN®

The Executioner

#152 Combat Stretch
#153 Firebase Florida
#154 Night Hit
#155 Hawaiian Heat
#156 Phantom Force
#157 Cayman Strike
#158 Firing Line
#159 Steel and Flame
#160 Storm Warning
#161 Eye of the Storm
#162 Colors of Hell
#163 Warrior's Edge
#164 Death Trail
#165 Fire Sweep
#166 Assassin's Creed
#167 Double Action
#168 Blood Price
#169 White Heat
#170 Baja Blitz
#171 Deadly Force
#172 Fast Strike
#173 Capitol Hit
#174 Battle Plan
#175 Battle Ground
#176 Ransom Run
#177 Evil Code
#178 Black Hand
#179 War Hammer
#180 Force Down
#181 Shifting Target
#182 Lethal Agent
#183 Clean Sweep
#184 Death Warrant
#185 Sudden Fury
#186 Fire Burst
#187 Cleansing Flame
#188 War Paint
#189 Wellfire
#190 Killing Range
#191 Extreme Force
#192 Maximum Impact
#193 Hostile Action
#194 Deadly Contest
#195 Select Fire
#196 Triburst
#197 Armed Force
#198 Shoot Down
#199 Rogue Agent
#200 Crisis Point
#201 Prime Target
#202 Combat Zone
#203 Hard Contact
#204 Rescue Run
#205 Hell Road
#206 Hunting Cry
#207 Freedom Strike
#208 Death Whisper
#209 Asian Crucible
#210 Fire Lash
#211 Steel Claws

DON PENDLETON'S

THE EXECUTIONER®

STEEL CLAWS

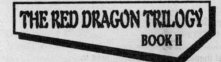

THE RED DRAGON TRILOGY
BOOK II

A GOLD EAGLE BOOK FROM
WORLDWIDE®

TORONTO • NEW YORK • LONDON
AMSTERDAM • PARIS • SYDNEY • HAMBURG
STOCKHOLM • ATHENS • TOKYO • MILAN
MADRID • WARSAW • BUDAPEST • AUCKLAND

First edition July 1996
ISBN 0-373-64211-3

Special thanks and acknowledgment to Mike Newton for his contribution to this work.

STEEL CLAWS

Printed in U.S.A.

There is justice, but we do not always see it. Discreet, smiling, it is there, at one side, a little bit behind injustice, which makes a big noise.

—Jules Renard

Justice is catching up to the bad guys, this time. It won't be pretty, it won't be smiling, and it's going to make one hell of a noise.

—Mack Bolan

THE MACK BOLAN® LEGEND

Nothing less than a war could have fashioned the destiny of the man called Mack Bolan. Bolan earned the Executioner title in the jungle hell of Vietnam.

But this soldier also wore another name—Sergeant Mercy. He was so tagged because of the compassion he showed to wounded comrades-in-arms and Vietnamese civilians.

Mack Bolan's second tour of duty ended prematurely when he was given emergency leave to return home and bury his family, victims of the Mob. Then he declared a one-man war against the Mafia.

He confronted the Families head-on from coast to coast, and soon a hope of victory began to appear. But Bolan had broken society's every rule. That same society started gunning for this elusive warrior—to no avail.

So Bolan was offered amnesty to work within the system against terrorism. This time, as an employee of Uncle Sam, Bolan became Colonel John Phoenix. With a command center at Stony Man Farm in Virginia, he and his new allies—Able Team and Phoenix Force—waged relentless war on a new adversary: the KGB.

But when his one true love, April Rose, died at the hands of the Soviet terror machine, Bolan severed all ties with Establishment authority.

Now, after a lengthy lone-wolf struggle and much soul-searching, the Executioner has agreed to enter an "arm's-length" alliance with his government once more, reserving the right to pursue personal missions in his Everlasting War.

1

Amsterdam

Holland's largest city had something for everyone, from classic art museums to war memorials, exotic dining, festivals and flower markets, ancient churches and ultramodern department stores.

For those in search of "special" action, there was Nieuwmarkt, which included the red-light district, sex shows, quasilegal hash bars and the largest Chinatown in Europe.

It was a yearning for Chinese that brought Mack Bolan into Nieuwmarkt on a Thursday night, when garish neon and low-lying clouds eclipsed the stars. He moved along the fragrant streets like any other tourist, smiling at the hookers who displayed themselves in lighted windows, and rubbed shoulders with the young and not-so-young who wandered in and out of small cafés that reeked of marijuana.

Unlike the others, though, he wore a sleek Beretta 93-R automatic slung beneath his left arm, with an Uzi submachine gun on a swivel rig below his right arm. His plain black raincoat hid the weapons, but he wore the coat unbuttoned to facilitate a fast draw if the need arose.

Considering its liberal drug laws and preeminence in foreign trade, it came as no surprise to anyone that Amsterdam was labeled the heroin capital of Europe. Chinese Triad

mobsters dominated the trade in Asian heroin, with Amsterdam doubling as a lucrative market and transshipment point. Hard drugs were technically illegal in the Netherlands, but Dutch police had publicly proclaimed that intercepting drugs in transit wasn't a priority. As for domestic junkies, their enslavement to the needle helped account for Holland's shocking crime rate, with a per capita victimization rate surpassing that of the United States, Great Britain, France or Italy.

You wouldn't know it, walking on the peaceful streets of Amsterdam—unless, perhaps, you took a wrong turn in the red-light district and wound up on one of the seedy side streets around Oude Zijde Voorburgwal.

The Chinese colony in Amsterdam was located on the northern edge of Nieuwmarkt, where an ancient sea dyke once protected Amsterdam from being flooded by the turbulent North Sea. A walk along those streets, adjacent to the red-light district, conjured echoes and aromas common to the Chinese neighborhoods of London, San Francisco, New York and a hundred other cities circling the globe: exotic restaurants and tourist shops, street signs in Cantonese and pharmacies that peddled powdered rhino horn and tiger's penis side by side with ginseng root and herbal teas.

As anywhere, the vast majority of Chinese residents in Amsterdam were peaceful, law-abiding folk, if somewhat reticent in dealing with the authorities. As anywhere, the proud community was also victimized by certain predators who focused more on profit than on brotherhood.

It was the predators whom Bolan sought this night. His quest had brought him to the Zhi-chuang Club, a gambling parlor owned and operated by a local family of the Triad known as the 14K.

It was, if nothing else, a place to start.

The Executioner had come to Amsterdam in earnest, and he hadn't come alone.

DAVID MCCARTER STOOD across the street from a small restaurant on Warmoesstraat and watched the soldiers trooping in and out. They weren't military men, per se; no uniforms or weapons were openly displayed, though most of them were surely armed. These soldiers served the 14K, and their commander was a Hong Kong refugee named Kin Yau. Their actions weren't advertised and rarely made the papers. They were no less deadly for their secrecy, however, and McCarter kept that fact in mind.

It was his second day in Amsterdam, and McCarter was glad to be moving at last. There had been no hitch in the pickup when he rendezvoused with Bolan in the terminal at Schipol Airport. Yakov Katzenelenbogen had been waiting in the car outside. The afternoon had been consumed with planning, sharing information, bringing one another up to speed. Now they were ready.

Anyhow, as ready as they'd ever be.

Three men against an army didn't make the best of odds, but it was always like that with Phoenix Force. They never drew a job where the U.S. Marines would do as well—black operations, hit-and-run, the kind of thing that Washington wasn't supposed to be involved in. Now, with three-fifths of the team sidetracked on other pressing business in Peru, Katz and McCarter would be backing Bolan's play in Amsterdam—and on from there, whatever happened next.

But for the moment McCarter's full attention focused on the restaurant that was his target. Owned and operated by the Chinese godfather of Amsterdam, it was a combination hangout for the troops, nerve center for dispensing information and convenient laundry for a portion of the money Yau raked in from the narcotics trade. Legitimate investments let the dirty cash remain in circulation, written off as restaurant receipts, and provided Yau with a facade of decency that served him well in the community at large.

McCarter reckoned it was time to shake things up a bit.

He crossed the street. One of his hands was inside the vertical slit pocket of his raincoat, wrapped around the pistol grip of his MP-5 K subgun. The stubby weapon, devoid of silencer, was supported on a shoulder sling. McCarter wanted noise when he cut loose inside the restaurant—no doubt about his purpose, no mixed signals to the enemy or innocent bystanders on the battleground.

Nobody tried to stop him at the door. The restaurant was popular with tourists who were ignorant of any underworld connections, satisfied to eat their food and share stale jokes about how they would all be hungry in an hour or so.

A smiling hostess offered to relieve McCarter of his coat, but he declined and asked to see the manager. She led him off to one side, skirting the main dining room, along a murky corridor to reach a tall green door. The woman knocked and waited, showing him a strained, uncertain version of her smile before the door was opened by a hard-eyed Triad gunner who peered through the crack.

McCarter wasted no time on formalities. He kicked the door with force enough to break the shooter's nose and cheekbone, following through before the other men inside the private office had a chance to wonder what was happening. The SMG was in his hand, its stubby muzzle covering the room at large and daring anyone to make a move.

The Briton had the time to count four soldiers standing, with an older man behind a cluttered desk, before it went to hell. One of the gunmen on his left was fading back, his right hand inside his jacket, and McCarter didn't have the time or inclination to negotiate. He held down the MP-5 K's trigger and swept the room, 9 mm bullets ripping into flesh and fabric as his human targets started twitching, reeling, going down.

He emptied the 30-round box magazine, then reloaded swiftly, conscious of the Chinese hostess screaming as she fled. The groggy soldier at his feet was struggling to rise and

fight, so McCarter drilled him with a 3-round burst at close to skin-touch range.

The Phoenix Force commando heard the reinforcements coming, but stood his ground and met them with a burst that dropped two soldiers in their tracks. A third man stumbled back and out of sight with bullets in his side and shoulder.

The dining room was chaos: women screaming, diners rushing for the exits, overturning chairs and tables as they fled, some of them slipping, sliding, sprawling in the spillage from their neighbors. On the far side of the room, a Triad soldier fired two pistol shots and missed McCarter by at least ten feet. The Briton let it go, merging with the exodus of customers, and made it to the street as half a dozen Triad gunners did their best to buck the tide to get back inside to help their comrades.

They were late this time, but something told McCarter they would have another chance before too long.

YAN KWONG LIT a cigarette, inhaling deeply, letting smoke spill from his nostrils as he checked his Rolex watch for the sixth or seventh time in half an hour. He was tired of sentry duty at the Zhi-chuang Club. The hours seemed to drag, and Kwong was bored.

Sometimes he almost wished that something bad *would* happen, just to shake things up and let him see some action. It was dreary, watching old men come and go around the mah-jongg tables, smoking their cigars and sipping liquor from tiny glasses. It reminded Kwong of working in a rest home. He had yet to draw the pistol that he wore concealed beneath his jacket, and the only "action" he had seen since his assignment to the club featured two men in their sixties arguing about a hand of cards, exchanging curses, waving bony fists. A schoolboy could have separated them, and in lieu of kicking ass, the proprietor dispensed free drinks to calm them.

Still, it was easy work, and Kwong had ample free time for the hash bars or some window-shopping in the red-light district when he wasn't propping up a wall and watching old men lose their money to the house. On the rare occasions that a debt was overdue and Kwong had to go collect the money or a pound of flesh, he never had trouble with the senior citizens. Their bones were brittle, muscles turning into flab, and it didn't require much energy to make them see the error of their ways in holding out on Kin Yau.

Kwong hadn't killed a man as yet, but he was looking forward to it. In the old days, he was told, bloodshed was part of the Triad initiation process. Every soldier had to prove himself, if not in battle, then with the assassination of some target chosen by his chief. More recently, while terrorism still remained a most effective tool in Chinatown, the emphasis was placed on monetary profits rather than displaying proof of manhood with a knife or gun.

Kwong sometimes read about the ancient tong wars and discussed the "good old days" with aging soldiers who had fought to make the 14K preeminent in Amsterdam, back in the early 1970s. A rival family from Singapore had claimed the city for its own, trying to control the flow of heroin from Southeast Asia, executing any challengers. Kin Yau had been the new kid on the block, the youngest red pole in the 14K, entrusted with a mission that would make or break his future with the Triad. It had taken three long, bloody years to rout the Singaporeans, but Yau had done the job. Now he was reaping the rewards of victory, relaxing in his forties, letting younger men—like Kwong—stand watch against potential enemies.

Except there seemed to be no enemies these days. A brief dispute with the Colombians, over the cocaine trade in Amsterdam, had been negotiated without bloodshed eight months earlier. No one was fool enough to challenge Kin Yau in Chinatown.

But there had been rumors the previous night of war in London. It was whispered that Wong Kam was dead, along with many of his soldiers, and the man or men responsible were unidentified. A tiny item in the newspaper referred to certain deaths in London's Chinatown, but there were no specifics, certainly no mention of the 14K.

And so Kwong almost hoped that something of the kind would happen in Amsterdam. He didn't want to die, but war would mean a break in the infernal tedium, a chance for him to prove himself. He was too young to fear a faceless enemy, regardless of the damage suffered by his brothers on some other battlefield.

Kwong took a last drag on his cigarette and moved in the direction of a standing sand-filled ashtray several paces to his left. The main room of the Zhi-chuang Club was fairly quiet aside from the sounds of riffling cards and clicking dominoes, the muted voices of old men exchanging stories they had told a thousand times before. A smoky haze hung in the air—tobacco smoke, no opium or marijuana was allowed on the premises.

Too bad, Kwong thought. If they made hash available...

Kwong lost his train of thought as he beheld a stranger entering the smoky gaming room from the direction of the storage area in back. The new arrival was a white man, tall and dark, well dressed in a stylish suit beneath the raincoat he wore. His cold eyes took in the whole room at a glance.

Kwong shot a hasty glance in the direction of his supervisor and quickly ascertained that Chang Lu hadn't seen the stranger yet. If this was a police raid, they should certainly have been warned. Kin Yau paid ample bribes to keep himself from any rude surprises, and—

The Uzi in the stranger's hands told Kwong that he was no policeman. This was trouble, and he had to act without delay; there was no time to ask Lu's advice.

Kwong reached inside his jacket for the pistol, felt it warm against his fingers as the Uzi swung in his direction, spitting fire.

It was the last thing Yan Kwong ever saw.

YAKOV KATZENELENBOGEN'S first grenade, tossed from a range of forty feet, was right on target. The painted window shattered, spilling light into the alley, and he ducked back as the fragmentation grenade went off.

Inside the cutting plant, confusion reigned.

Katz counted off three seconds, waiting for the storm of shrapnel to subside, then left the fire escape and entered the building through the shattered window. He wore a gas mask to protect himself from smoke, dust and the drifting cloud of uncut heroin that his grenade had whipped up in the loft.

The cutting plant was one of six or seven operated by the 14K in Amsterdam. On any given day, it turned a dozen kilos of the finest China white into a *hundred* kilos cut and ready for the streets. That meant a profit markup of some two thousand percent for Yau, who bought the uncut poison at a special discount from his Triad brothers in the Golden Triangle and shipped it out from Bangkok or Hong Kong. Allowing for Yau's overhead, including payoffs to police and customs agents, that still left a profit margin to the 14K approaching seven million dollars per month. The Dutch government's network of supervised narcotic-distribution centers for registered addicts had shaved a few bucks off the top, but there was still enough underground traffic to keep Yau and his family well funded through the next century.

Katz had a laser sight mounted underneath the muzzle of his Uzi SMG to help him pick out targets in the swirling haze. A couple of the big fluorescent fixtures overhead had been destroyed by shrapnel from his frag grenade, and the surviving lights were flickering like candles in a fitful breeze.

He scanned the room and saw wreckage where the blast had flipped a long and heavy wooden table over on its side. Equipment from the cutting plant was strewed across the floor: digital scales, a drift of plastic sandwich bags, spoons and knives, some broken dishes, heroin and baking soda heaped together on the vinyl floor. It felt like walking on a beach, the powder grating underfoot, but Katz was busy seeking targets. He could always clean his shoes another time.

Two bodies lay on the floor immediately to his left. Both male, he recognized, despite the surgical masks they wore, since both were stripped to undershorts. It was the standard uniform for cutting plants, where the proprietors were more concerned with possible employee theft than the havoc they were wreaking on society.

One of the workers was unconscious, maybe dead, blood streaming from an ugly scalp wound. His companion tried to rise, still dazed from the blast, but Katzenelenbogen kicked him in the face and put him down again. The kick dislodged his target's mask and left him sucking uncut scag in volumes that would kill a horse.

A sound of shuffling footsteps to Katz's right swung him in that direction, following the Uzi's lead. The red dot of his laser sight fixed on a flat, round face, eyes glaring at him above a crooked surgical mask. This man was fully dressed, a watchdog, groping for the pistol that he wore beneath his dusty jacket.

Katz stroked the Uzi's trigger, slicing the gunman's face off with a burst that pitched him over backward. There would be other sentries on the premises, Katz knew, and he would have to be alert for any who had come through the initial blast intact.

Outside and down the hall he heard somebody shouting. He didn't speak the language and had no way of knowing whether it was one of Yau's soldiers or a neighbor shaken by the sounds of combat. Either way it meant that rein-

forcements would be coming—either Triad troops or the police—and Katz wasn't prepared to deal with either if they came at him in heavy numbers.

Time to go, but first he finished checking out the room. A second gunman huddled in the corner, groping for a weapon he had lost when the grenade went off. Katz kicked the pistol over toward his cringing adversary, waiting while the Chinese gunman saw his last, dim chance and went for it. The Uzi stuttered, slamming half a dozen parabellum rounds into the rag-doll figure before he got his automatic off the floor.

The third and final soldier had been killed by shrapnel, laid out on his back with glassy eyes fixed on the ceiling overhead. The rest were workers, dazed or wounded, and two of them were already twitching through the final stages of an overdose from breathing uncut China white without their masks.

Katz left them to it, wished them all the good luck they deserved. Outside he kept his mask on as he scrambled down the fire escape, then took time to dust his clothes off in the alley. Tucking his Uzi out of sight, he started back in the direction of his car.

Not bad.

And they were only getting started, still in the initial phases of their strike.

The best, he knew, was yet to come.

THE TRIAD SOLDIER went down kicking, gutted by a burst from Bolan's Uzi, flopping like a grounded trout across a floor already slick with blood. Those first rounds from the Executioner's SMG brought panic to the Zhi-chuang Club, with players scrambling from their seats and overturning tables as they tried to reach the nearest exit, running for their lives.

This kind of interruption obviously didn't happen every day in Chinatown, but the surviving gunners held their

ground like pros. The three men were staked out at the remaining corners of the room, prepared to nail their round-eyed adversary with triangulated fire. It was a good defensive plan, and Bolan had to dive for cover as they opened up in unison, their bullets chipping at the redbrick walls.

He landed on his stomach, knees and elbows pumping as he sought the cover of a capsized mah-jongg table. Scattered tiles and money slithered out from under him as Bolan found his meager sanctuary, keeping low to duck the bullets that had followed him and were already hammering the table.

Sitting still was suicide, he realized. The gunners had all night to pepper him with bullets, and it wouldn't take that long for them to shred the table, riddle it with holes and nail him where he lay, concealed but hardly out of range. It galled him, being stuck on the defensive in the early moments of his probe, and Bolan knew that there was more than pride at stake. His very life was riding on the line, unless he seized control of the unstable situation and reversed the odds.

The Executioner poked his SMG around a corner of the table, firing blind, to keep his opposition on their toes. No lucky hit that time, but he wasn't expecting one. It was a diversion, something to prevent them from rushing him while he was reaching underneath his raincoat to extract a stun grenade.

The stunner—what police sometimes referred to as a flash-bang—was designed to render enemies unconscious or disabled without lasting injury. The Executioner had clipped one to his belt before he left his car, with thoughts of the casino's clientele in mind. Civilian casualties weren't part of his game plan, and it sounded as if a few stray customers were still pinned down between the Triad gunners and his own position, crying out in fear each time the guns went off.

He couldn't target all three gunners with the same grenade, but if he played his cards right, it would still distract

them, maybe blind them or at least stretch their reaction time enough to give him a fighting chance.

He yanked the safety pin and made the pitch without a clear fix on his targets, angling for a point across the room and near the middle of the floor. He heard the stunner hit and roll, one of the gunners calling out some kind of warning to his friends before their time ran out.

He kept his eyes closed and missed the blinding flash of light, but Bolan's ears were ringing as he vaulted to his feet. There was no time to waste, since the effects of the grenade depended on proximity.

The Triad gunner on his left was closest—which meant farthest from the blast—and Bolan nailed him first, a rising 6-round burst that stitched him from his groin up to his larynx, slammed him back against the nearest wall and left a crimson smear behind him as he slid down to the floor.

The gunner at the apex of the triangle was nearest to the blast and seemed to be unconscious, stretched out on the floor. His sidekick, off to Bolan's right, was scrubbing at his eyes with one hand, while the other squeezed off aimless bullets from a shiny automatic pistol. The Executioner shot him in the chest, four rounds to put the soldier down and keep him there, then swung back toward the middle man, still sprawled out on the floor, unmoving.

Let it go.

It wouldn't hurt for him to leave a witness who could spread the word among his fellows, maybe wreaking havoc with morale. The soldier would describe a round-eyed adversary, and Kin Yau would ultimately draw connections with the past week's violence in London, New York City, San Francisco and Vancouver.

Fine.

It wouldn't hurt to lay the cards out on the table, Bolan thought, and let his enemies imagine what was coming next.

Besides, the Executioner still had some aces up his sleeve.

Lieutenant Jan van Straten of the Amsterdam police department's drug and vice division watched as paramedics brought another shrouded corpse out of the Zhi-chuang Club and stowed it in the waiting ambulance. Three dead, plus one unconscious and a handful who complained of minor injuries, including bruises and abrasions, headaches and bloody noses.

And the detective knew it could have been much worse.

It *was* worse, several blocks away, at Yung Fat's restaurant, where half a dozen men were dead. Worse yet at the illegal cutting plant, a short walk to the south, with shrapnel, gunshot wounds and overdoses in a kind of grisly competition to see which would finish off the ten employees there.

Straten had already been inside the Zhi-chuang Club. He knew it was an outlaw gambling establishment, protected by a combination of tradition and strategic bribes. Unlicensed and restricted to a Chinese clientele, it offered no real competition to the great Holland Casino Amsterdam, in the Hilton Hotel on Apollolaan, where tourists gladly gave their money to the house. No one complained if the Chinese amused themselves in Chinatown... unless it started getting bloody, as it had this night.

Straten knew there would be no arrests for gambling, even so. The laissez-faire approach to law enforcement ruled in Amsterdam, where prostitution, live-sex shows, hard drugs

and child pornography were all proscribed by law, but no one gave a damn. As long as the illegal business was conducted quietly, with no disturbance of the peace, police had more-important things to do. And since the vilest murderer could only be imprisoned for a short term in Holland under the prevailing law, there was no great incentive to pursue arrests on charges that would mostly be thrown out of court in any case.

It sometimes frustrated Straten when he thought about his job, the fifteen years he had invested in the abstract game of law and order. The wealthy merchant class of free-and-easy Amsterdam complained if pushers sold their wares too openly, outside the better shops, but those same "civic leaders" championed the red-light district as a tourist draw that helped make everybody rich. Except the junkies, hookers and compulsive gamblers, of course...but who were they, and who was interested in what became of them?

Aware that drug addiction led directly to the vast majority of muggings, burglaries, assaults and robberies investigated by police in any given year, Straten blamed the Chinese Triad for the lion's share of crime in Amsterdam. Without cocaine and heroin, the Dutch crime rate would never have surpassed America's or Britain's, as it had consistently in recent years. No racist, the lieutenant recognized that there were predators and thieves in any ethnic group, but there had been no underground drug culture in the Netherlands, no syndicated crime to speak of, in the years before the Triads came.

And there was nothing he could do about it now.

Straten watched the ambulance depart—no flashing lights or wailing siren for the dead—and wondered if his scheduled meet with the American would shed some light on what was happening, perhaps suggest a tentative solution to the problem. It was doubtful, granted, but Straten lived with hope. As cynical and jaded as his job had made him, the lieutenant still had moments when he hoped to glimpse a

dim light at the tunnel's end, to know that justice had been served.

Fat chance.

The meet had been arranged by Captain Dekker, on his own initiative. No explanation, just an address and the order to appear, meet the American and cooperate if possible.

There was some trouble with the Triads in the States. What else was new? Straten knew about the recent shooting match in London, too, and wondered if it was somehow connected to the sudden deaths in Amsterdam. A gang war was the last thing anybody needed, but Straten wouldn't mind too much if some of Kin Yau's soldiers went to their reward. And if the red pole bought it, too, well, that would be a shame.

Like hell.

He checked his watch and saw that it was almost time to keep his date with Mike Belasko, from America. A pseudonym, no doubt, but it was better than the normal "Smith" or "Jones" routine he got from the DEA.

Straten lit a cigarette and turned back toward his car.

It wouldn't do to keep an ally waiting, after all.

IT HAD BEEN thirteen years since Kin Yau had murdered with his own two hands. He had an army to perform his dirty work these days, and it was rare that problems went so far as to require a death sentence. The past two years his men had executed only four men that Yau could recall, and three of those had been Colombians who broke the trade agreement Yau had signed with Medellín by poaching in his own backyard.

He was a man of peace, the chief philanthropist of Chinatown, well-known among his people as a patron of the arts. Of course, they feared him—that was only proper—but he didn't wield the power he possessed in vengeful or haphazard fashion. Yau bent over backward, in his own view,

to accommodate his own and the community of Amsterdam at large.

All things considered, then, the flurry of attacks against his men were even more despicable. The men responsible would have to be found and punished for their insolence. A red pole who allowed himself to be insulted in the public eye would quickly lose respect, and that meant he would ultimately lose control.

It was a fact that Tu Sheng had tried to warn him. He'd flown in from London with his tail between his legs and babbled on about the troubles there, how Wong Kam and his soldiers had been massacred by round-eyes from America. It made no sense, and Yau had chosen to ignore the problem, let his brothers in the U.S.A. and Britain deal with matters in their own preserves. He still had no proof that the raids in Amsterdam were related to attacks in England or the States, but it defied coincidence that Yau would find himself besieged so quickly after his associates had come under fire and failed to properly defend themselves.

He had to do better than the others; that was obvious. He wouldn't contemplate defeat. It was preposterous. Unthinkable. His soldiers were the best, though many of them had never faced determined enemies of flesh and blood. Still, they were willing, able, armed and ready. They would fight and die as necessary, for the honor of the 14K.

He thought of calling Sheng, then dismissed the notion. The last thing Yau needed at the moment was some mainlander's "I told you so," when he had work to do and enemies to kill.

Besides, Sheng would find out the bad news soon enough. He merely had to turn on the television or listen to the radio. Perhaps he would be frightened, run away again as he had done in London. It would be amusing to observe the Dragon's insolent ambassador in flight, as if he were a child.

In fact it might redeem an otherwise pathetic day.

While he was waiting for the mainlander to run, though, Yau had work to do. Somewhere in Amsterdam his enemies were scheming, looking for another opportunity to stab him in the back. He had to be ready for them when it happened, have his soldiers on alert and prepared for anything. It wouldn't do for him to be caught napping when an empire was at stake.

Already they had cost him men and money. It wasn't disastrous yet, but Yau could ill afford such treatment at the hands of strangers. Round-eyes yet. That made the insult all the more humiliating.

He knew that much from survivors at the Zhi-chuang Club and Yung Fat's restaurant. White men had done this to him, placed him in a situation where he had to take arms and defend himself against invaders for the first time in two decades.

Why? He neither knew nor cared. Consideration of an adversary's motive only helped if you were leaning toward negotiation—which Yau wasn't—and then only if you knew his name. In this case, where he was the victim of a brutal sneak attack, the only fair response was overwhelming force.

And still Yau's problem was the same. He couldn't strike back at his enemies until he found out who and where they were. It was impossible to fight a war with shadows and expect to win. The fact that his opponents were Caucasian hampered Yau, in that his eyes and ears were mainly concentrated in the area of Chinatown. Not solely—that would be a serious mistake—but it would take both finesse and cash to draw the necessary information from police... assuming they knew anything to tell.

Yau poured himself a double shot of gin and concentrated on the problem, thinking hard. For every riddle there was a solution. All he had to do was find it, soon.

In time to save his empire and his life.

THE DUTCH REFERRED to them as "brown cafés," those rough equivalent of English pubs that served three meals a day, along with native gin and other potables. The name derived from polished wood interiors, low-wattage lighting and the residue of nicotine imparted by generations of enthusiastic smokers. Spartan decor was the rule of thumb, with no upholstery or cushions on the furniture, although some brown cafés sported well-worn Persian rugs atop their tables to absorb spilled beer. The walls were generally bare of art or other decoration, save for calendars that were as likely to be out-of-date as current.

Seated in the rearmost corner of a brown café on Zeedijk, Bolan sipped his pint of beer and waited for the Dutch policeman to arrive. It was a chancy moment, meeting someone who could just as easily betray him as assist his cause. He had no way of knowing what the lawman had been told by his superiors, or whether private attitudes would make the meet a waste of time. A false step, here and now, could ruin everything.

He recognized the cop at once by type, despite the fact that they had never met and no description had been offered in advance: the old world-weariness around his eyes that came from seeing too much death and degradation in the line of duty, furrows carved in sunburned cheeks by the habitual frown.

His guest spied Bolan, a silent signal passing between them, and he stopped off at the bar to get a glass of gin before he made his way back to the narrow booth.

"Mr. Belasko?"

"In the flesh. And you are...?"

"Jan van Straten, first lieutenant, narcotics and vice division. What brings you to Amsterdam?"

"The 14K."

"I should have guessed. You've had some trouble with them recently in the United States, I think."

"The trouble cuts both ways," Bolan said.

"Mmm. Indeed." The lawman sipped his gin. "You're far from home, in any case."

"The men I'm after don't like sitting still."

"There are procedures," Straten said. "Surely you know that."

"Of course. That's why I'm touching base."

"What can I do for you?"

"Are you familiar with a Chinese named Tu Sheng?" Bolan asked.

"That one!" Straten made a sour face. "He plays the part of a respected lower-level diplomat, holds meetings with some undersecretary now and then to talk about the prospects for increasing trade with mainland China. On the side he spends a great deal of his time with members of the Triads, doing God knows what. If I were a suspicious man, I might think someone in Beijing was looking for a treaty with the 14K."

"You wouldn't be far wrong."

"I thought as much. Of course, we can't touch Sheng. He's got the standard diplomatic cover, and there's no hard evidence of any criminal activity. So there is no great incentive to investigate a foreign diplomat who can't be legally detained in any case."

"I wasn't planning to arrest him," Bolan said.

"Oh, no?"

"Strictly speaking I'm not a policeman. More of a soldier, really."

"Ah. And has the U.S.A. declared war on the Triads, then?"

"You won't find anything on paper."

"Plausible deniability," Straten said. "I have the term correctly?"

"Close enough."

"It's not the way we do things here in Amsterdam. I'm not sure why my captain wanted us to meet."

"I'm not recruiting soldiers," Bolan said, "but I could use some information from a man who knows the area."

"What sort of information did you have in mind?"

"A better list of Kin Yau's properties than what I have. More importantly a lead on Sheng. Someplace where I can find him if I need to, day or night."

Straten thought about it, finishing his gin and frowning. "You'd make me an accomplice to assassination, then."

"Depends on how you look at things. One way to think of it is that you're helping flush the scum out of your town."

"Suppose you fail?" Straten asked.

"My problem. You won't be in the line of fire, and no one gets your name from me."

Straten thought about it for another moment, then finally cracked a smile. "It's thirsty work, remembering these details," he remarked. "I'd better have another drink."

THE NEWS HAD GONE from bad to worse, and Tu Sheng was on the verge of desperation, pacing in his apartment on Waalsteeg like a tiger in a too-small cage. He recognized the symptoms, but he had no antidote. The fear was stifling, and no solution came to mind, no matter how he racked his brain.

He was supposed to be secure in Amsterdam, protected from the kind of madness that had threatened him in London—was it only yesterday? It felt to Sheng as if the ordeal had dragged on for days or even weeks. He hated hiding like a fugitive, despised himself for cowardice and worried what the others had to be thinking of him even now.

No matter.

It wasn't *his* place to prowl around the streets and shoot at people in the dark. If anyone confused him with a soldier, it was his mistake, not Sheng's. His mission was to supervise the 14K, coordinate its dealings with the Dragon and make sure that everything ran smoothly overseas.

In that regard, at least, the past two days had been disastrous. Sheng hadn't communicated with the Dragon since his flight to Amsterdam, and it wasn't a pleasant prospect now, with new attacks, new violence to report. Of course, he knew that none of it was his fault; anyone with common sense would recognize that fact, but Sheng was also well aware that setbacks of this nature called for the assignment of responsibility. That sometimes meant selection of a scapegoat if the real culprit wasn't identified.

But Sheng was no man's scapegoat, no pathetic whipping boy. He wouldn't willingly accept a stain upon his reputation when he knew that he wasn't to blame for what had happened.

He was innocent.

The trick, he realized, would be to sell the Dragon on that notion, make it stick and so protect himself from sharp knives in the back.

Before he puzzled over that prospect, however, there was a more pressing item on his mind. In London he had narrowly escaped assassination by the round-eyes who were persecuting members of the 14K in North America and Europe. He assumed the CIA had to be involved, but who was responsible was less important at the moment than survival.

Dead men didn't have to think about their reputations, after all.

Sheng peered out through his window, one eye peeping through a two-inch gap in heavy curtains. There was nothing on the street below to indicate that he was being watched, but would he see his enemies before they struck?

Wong Kam had been prepared for anything in London, but it hadn't saved him. He was dead now, with at least two dozen of his soldiers who had failed to keep their red pole safe from harm.

Sheng had no soldiers of his own, instead relying on his "comrades" in the 14K to manage his security if there was

any need. Right now he had two young men sitting in his living room, their pistols on his coffee table as they smoked cigarettes and watched some X-rated garbage on the television. Sheng supposed they were professional enough, but what could two men do when twenty-five or thirty weren't enough in London, New York, San Francisco and Vancouver?

Given half a chance, he would have run for home, but Sheng knew how the Dragon would react to that. There would be no appeal, no explanation for deserting under fire. An order to evacuate was one thing, but if *he* departed on his own initiative, Sheng knew he was as good as dead.

The next-best thing was to remain in hiding, wait to see which way the storm winds blew in Amsterdam. There was a chance that Yau would manage to defeat these round-eyes, when his brothers of the 14K had failed. In that case Sheng would celebrate the victory, and they could all get back to business as usual.

And if it went the other way...

He didn't like to think about that prospect. Visions of his own mortality weren't inclined to lift Sheng's spirits or imbue him with enthusiasm for his job. In fact these past two days, he had begun to doubt the People's Revolution for the first time in his life.

Too late for that, of course. His path was set, and there was no escape from destiny. Sheng might not be a soldier, but he still waged war against the Western adversaries in his own way. He was a vital member of the Dragon's team, not easily replaced.

Or so he hoped.

If he was wrong, there would be hell to pay.

"I THOUGHT WE'D SPLIT the list three ways," Bolan said.

He was seated on the bed in his hotel room at the Trianon, on Brouersstraat. Katz and McCarter faced him, both

men holding to a military posture in their straight-backed wooden chairs.

"The cop came through?" McCarter asked.

"A dozen possibles," Bolan replied, "plus an address for my buddy Tu Sheng."

"You want to take him first?" Katzenelenbogen asked.

Bolan thought about it for a moment, then finally shook his head. "I'd like to rattle Kin Yau's cage a little more. Give everybody in his family a chance to feel the heat."

"And after Amsterdam?" McCarter asked.

"Depends. I'm working back along the pipeline toward the source. We've got a whole list of deserving targets if we get that far. Let's take it one step at a time."

"You're biting off a mouthful." Katz didn't sound discouraged, but there was a note of caution in his tone.

"The 14K's been growing like a weed," Bolan said, "everywhere you look. They've got the family tree in Washington, chapter and verse, but no one's really laid a glove on them so far. Now, with the diplomatic angle, there's a chance nobody ever will. We can't allow that."

"No," McCarter said, "but when you talk about the 14K, you're talking... what? Some thirty thousand guns?"

"I didn't plan to face them all at once."

"There's still the law of averages," Katz stated.

"Agreed. That's why we take it one step at a time and see what happens next. I've never cared much for the kamikaze style of warfare."

Katz ran a finger down the list he had received from Bolan. "I saw this place today. It looked respectable enough."

"What else is new?" the Executioner replied. "Kin Yau's had twenty years to cover his tracks in Amsterdam. That's one thing on our side. I think he's gotten soft."

"How many soldiers overall?" McCarter asked.

"A hundred, give or take," Bolan replied. "We've reduced the count by ten percent already."

"Reinforcements?" Katz queried.

"With London out of action for the moment," Bolan said, "his best bet would be France. The 14K has people there, but nothing on the scale of Amsterdam. They have to deal with competition from the Corsicans. It still gets sticky every now and then."

"That's good to know," McCarter said.

"Could be. Is everybody set in terms of hardware?"

"Fine," Katz said.

"I'm happy," McCarter added.

"Great. Let's grab a bite and hit the bricks."

He understood the reservations of his Phoenix Force allies, felt the same constraints himself. The odds were overwhelming if they hesitated long enough to check out the big picture; thirty thousand dedicated soldiers of the 14K lined up to take them out. But Bolan had come this far alone, and now the three of them were even better able to contend with killer odds.

As long as they were careful, stuck within the limits of a high-risk game where everybody's life was riding on the line.

The struggle had to be taken one day at a time, or it would break a man's spirit, drive him crazy with the certain knowledge that his adversaries had a bottomless reserve of predators to draw upon when there were vacancies to fill. As long as man had been a thinking animal, there had been predators on tap to terrorize the "civilized," and that would never change unless some laboratory found a cure for human nature. Even then, Bolan thought, the men who found the "cure" would almost certainly be angling for control, a bigger, better slice of pie.

The best that he could hope for was to stop their adversaries here, and then move on to seek another battlefield, repeat the process time and time again in hopes that it would stick someday.

The warehouse on Prins Hendrikkade was owned by Kin Yau through buffer companies that kept his name well insulated from investigators. It wasn't a perfect screen, but it had served him well enough for seven years. The fact that Amsterdam police had documented ownership within the past twelve months didn't suggest that Yau would suffer raids or any undue scrutiny around the warehouse. He behaved himself in public, there was nothing to suggest that anyone was being murdered on the premises and the police had other, more important fish to fry.

David McCarter, on the other hand, was very interested in what went on behind those doors. The former SAS commando had good reason to suspect that heroin, cocaine, illegal Chinese immigrants and other contraband arrived at Yau's warehouse both by truck and by canal boat. He didn't have to prove it in the sense of satisfying judges, juries or specific rules of evidence. It was enough for him to know Yau owned the property, and the man was designated as his target of the moment.

He parked next door, one car among two dozen in the lot outside a warehouse catering to frozen seafood. Walking back to Yau's place, he had time to double-check the compact submachine gun underneath his coat and the pistol slung beneath his left arm in a fast-draw rig.

The warehouse door was open and unguarded—so much for security. He stepped inside and let it close softly behind

him, waiting while his eyes grew accustomed to the change in light. A sound of voices speaking Cantonese led him along a corridor where careless footsteps would have echoed loudly, but he watched his step. A sharp turn to his left, and he was looking at the warehouse proper, with a small enclosure designated as the office to his right. Plywood partitions were finished off with glass above waist level, and the entryway was without a door. Four men took up most of the space, one of them pointing to a ledger that lay open on a cluttered desk, gesticulating with a zeal that could have indicated anger or enthusiasm for his job.

All four of those inside the office were Chinese, and three of them wore guns that weren't supposed to show beneath their sport coats.

Checking out the main space of the warehouse, McCarter saw no other signs of human life, no workmen to concern him when he set the place on fire.

He blocked the office doorway with his body, cleared his throat to let the Triads know they weren't alone and gave them time to glimpse his SMG. Two of them went for guns, and that was all he needed. He swept them from right to left and back again, the MP-5 K stitching them with hot 9 mm rounds. There was no place to hide in the restricted office space, and all four went down in seconds flat, blood pooling on the floor beneath them.

That left the warehouse, and McCarter did his business quickly, placing each of the four thermite canisters where it would do the ultimate in damage when it blew. He had no way of knowing what was in the crates, and he didn't care. The merchandise, legitimate or otherwise, would cost Yau money to replace, and that was part of bleeding him before the final killing stroke. Debilitate his operation, strike on several fronts at once, and it would all come crashing down.

In theory, anyway.

If they were wrong, McCarter told himself, there could be hell to pay.

THE SNIPER RIFLE WAS a folding-stock Galil, chambered in 7.62 mm, with a 20-round box magazine and a Nimrod six-power telescopic sight. The built-in bipod offered more stability than Bolan would have had if he was firing free-hand, and the stock was fitted with a rubber recoil pad. A specialized version of the standard Israeli service rifle, the Galil scored consistently inside an eleven-inch circle at six hundred meters—almost five times the range of Bolan's target from the firing point. The bulky silencer would shave a bit of muzzle energy, but that was fine.

The office occupied a fifth-floor corner space, northwest across Ilperveldestraat. From Bolan's rooftop aerie, with the Nimrod scope, he had a clear view of the office: some expensive-looking watercolors on the wall; a telephone constructed in the antique style, which looked as if it were made of gold and ivory; oak furnishings hand polished to a mirror shine. It was conspicuous consumption all the way.

The man behind the massive desk wasn't Kin Yau, but he would do. Yau's second-in-command was fielding calls despite the hour, and three men ringed his desk in captain's chairs, as if awaiting orders to depart and essay some heroic feat to please their master.

They'd get their chance now, Bolan thought as his warm cheek pressed against the cool wood of the sniper rifle's stock. His index finger curled around the trigger, taking up the slack until he felt resistance, knowing that another pound or so of pressure would unleash a screaming round downrange to shatter glass, rend flesh and bone.

He watched as Yau's lieutenant dropped the telephone receiver back into its cradle and began to lecture his small audience. The others nodded, puppetlike, but didn't speak. It would be rash to interrupt, a bad career move all the way.

In Bolan's case, however, he had no job to protect and he was bent on interrupting with a vengeance. Any second now.

He shifted to the nearest of the flunkies, zeroed on the nodding profile, made allowances for elevation and the

standard drop of a projectile traveling one hundred meters at a downward angle, which he estimated at fifteen degrees.

The Executioner took a breath and held it, leaned into the weapon as he squeezed the trigger gently and felt the rifle kick against his shoulder. The office window rippled, sprouted spiderweb designs.

His target lurched, blood spouting from the ruin of his face, and started sliding from his chair down to the floor. Before he made it, Bolan had a second face framed in his cross hairs, squeezing off again. There was no time for them to think or comprehend exactly what was happening before a second corpse lay stretched out on the deep-pile carpeting.

The two survivors were moving as he tracked them with his scope. The guy behind the desk had better possibilities for cover, so the next round went to him, a trifle hastily. It dropped slightly, ripping through his larynx rather than his face. It did the job, regardless, blood exploding from the man's jugular and his carotid artery. The impact spun him in his swivel chair and dumped him out of sight behind the desk, but he was done, unless somebody got him to a trauma center in the next two minutes flat.

And that left one.

The soldier had a fair start toward the door, and Bolan helped him along with a well-placed round between the shoulder blades. His running target vaulted forward, like a long jumper going for Olympic gold, and slammed face-first into the office door. A smudge of crimson marked the point where nasal cartilage met wood and came off second best.

Bolan spent a moment breaking down the rifle, stowed it in an olive drab duffel bag and slung the bag across his shoulder. Heading down the service stairs, he half expected someone to confront him—the apartment building's super, possibly a tenant, but he got out clean. Two blocks later he

reached his car, by which time he could see a handful of pedestrians collected on the sidewalk way downrange, examining the broken windows overhead and talking, no doubt, about the meaning of it all.

How long before somebody called the cops?

No matter. He was on his way, unnoticed, moving toward the next mark on his hit list. Katzenelenbogen and McCarter would be on a roll, with any luck their paths converging toward the final target that would bring them all together for the coup de grace in Amsterdam.

The war was far from over, but the battle was progressing well enough.

THE LATEST NEWS struck Kin Yau like a resounding slap across the face. He didn't mourn for Sin-Kiong Yu, but the man had been a valuable lieutenant, good with men and money—an unusual combination in the world Yau occupied. Replacing him would take some careful thought, and at the moment he was totally preoccupied with finding out who had pulled the trigger.

The raids against his sundry operations were continuing, and Yau still had no idea who was responsible, beyond the fact that various survivors said his enemies were white men. Not Colombians, from the description; more like Western Europeans or Americans. Yau thought immediately of the Mafia, perhaps the Corsicans, but they had all signed treaties with the 14K some time ago. A band of renegades, perhaps, intent on poaching Yau's narcotics territory?

No.

Competitors would concentrate on earning money first, and there had been no indication of unlicensed peddlers on his turf. There had to be some other motive, then . . . but what?

Revenge was something Yau could understand, and he had enemies enough to fill a good-sized auditorium, but most of them were fellow Asians, some Hispanics, one or

two disgruntled Turks. He hadn't been to the United States in seven years, and there had been no trouble at the time, a simple pleasure trip, with minor business meetings on the side. Yau's business took him into London several times a year, but none of the Caucasian gangs was large or bold enough to challenge him in Amsterdam.

Who, then, and why?

He slammed the desktop with his fist once more because the pain helped ease his rage. It galled Yau to sit behind a desk and wait for fresh news of disaster while some unknown adversary ran amok in Amsterdam, killed his employees, vandalized his property and burned up precious merchandise. Much more of this, and he would be a laughingstock among his troops and the Chinese community at large.

But what to do?

His contacts in the Amsterdam police department had been worse than useless so far. They were scurrying around behind the faceless gunmen, cleaning up their mess and interviewing Chinese witnesses who wouldn't willingly provide a lawman with the time of day. Officially it was suspected that the raids were staged by "criminals or terrorists." For all the insight their analysis contained, they might as well have said Yau's troops were shot by "men with guns."

Of course the lightning raids were carried out by criminals. Of course they aimed at terrorizing Kin Yau, but to what end? There had been no demands for tribute, territory or the like. No threats had been received, no messages of any kind, in fact. Survivors could recall no conversation with the gunmen who appeared and disappeared so readily on Yau's home turf. Whatever they intended for him, it was still a closely guarded secret kept among themselves.

That made it all the worse, of course. Yau understood the base emotions—lust, hate, envy, greed—that motivated people in his world. If this had been a blood feud or a war

for territory, he would understand...and he would also more than likely recognize his enemies. It was unprecedented for a group of white men to attack the 14K in Chinatown. Yau's last war, with the Singaporeans, had been a fratricidal interlude that never really fazed the Dutch community at large.

A race war, though... Well, that was something else.

Authorities would feel a greater need to intervene if there was any risk of white men getting killed. A threat to local tourism would be the worst scenario, and Yau could expect some repercussions if the violence took a bite out of the city's pocketbook.

With luck and fortune on his side, Yau knew it wouldn't have to go that far. Once he identified his enemies, they could be isolated, hunted down and made to disappear. It wouldn't be the first time or the last that he made problems go away, vanish without a trace.

And if it didn't go that smoothly, if his adversaries fought tenaciously, died in some public place, the media would soon forget about it. There would always be some fresh sensation, scandal or disaster waiting to monopolize the short attention span of a pathetic round-eyed audience. This time next week the public would be more concerned with some movie star's love life or the rising price of gasoline than with the fate of gunmen from a foreign country who had met their long-awaited doom in Amsterdam.

Yau sat back in his chair and made a conscious effort to relax. His enemies had had the upper hand so far, but they would soon run out of steam, and when that happened, it would be his turn.

KATZ LET THE CHINESE sentry see him. The Israeli was an old man, shuffling awkwardly along the alley west of Zeedijk, nothing for a strong young Triad soldier to regard as a potential danger. Maybe he was drunk or just decrepit, but he posed no threat in either case.

The fact that Kin Yau's lieutenants were concerned enough to post a guard outside the back door of the Jueding Club, where there would normally be none, told Katz something. Inside, the live-sex shows would be continuing, the players heedless of the fact that they were screwing in a war zone, but the men in charge were learning from their early losses.

Not enough so far, but they were working on it.

Katz was even with the sentry now. He faked a sudden fit of coughing, doubled over, knowing the man would make no move to help him. No help was required. His left hand found the Browning automatic underneath his jacket, and he thumbed off the safety, turning toward the lookout as he drew his weapon from its shoulder rig. The silencer reduced the noise of the report to something like a muffled sneeze, and Katz stepped in to catch the young man as he fell.

Inside, the air was heavy with tobacco smoke and musk, the sweaty smell of sex. Four paces brought him to the backstage area, where he could peer out at the all-male audience beyond the naked bodies coupling on a mattress planted in the middle of the stage. It didn't take a truckload of imagination, and the choreography was nonexistent, but the voyeurs in the audience were getting what they paid for. Later, if they didn't lose their edge to alcohol or hash, a short walk to the west would put them in the middle of the red-light district, where their fantasies could come to life in other ways.

But not tonight.

Katz primed a compact smoke grenade and rolled it underneath the nearby curtains, backing off before it popped and sizzled, spewing out ten thousand cubic feet of smoke. He didn't need a translator to know the customers were yelling "Fire!" as they stampeded for the exits, cursing, jostling one another in a panic as they ran.

So far so good.

Katz found a pair of Chinese sluggers closing on him, shouting in Cantonese at first, then switching to Dutch as they discovered he was white. The Uzi took them by surprise, sliding out from underneath his coat like magic and locking into target acquisition.

It was all downhill from there.

They tried to break in opposite directions, pro-style, but they never had the chance. The Uzi stuttered discreetly, tagging the guy on Katz's left and spinning him like a top. Before his body hit the floor, the second gunner was already jerking, spouting blood from blowholes in his chest and belly, tangling in the nearby curtains as he fell.

It was a short walk to the office, with no more opposition on the way. Katz found the harried-looking manager just clearing out, and shoved him back inside. A sharp jab from the Uzi's muzzle stifled any protest as the man slumped against his desk.

"Speak English?" Katz inquired.

"I do."

"How badly do you want to live?"

"I'm sorry?"

"Don't apologize," Katz snapped, "just answer. Do you want to live or die?"

His captive didn't need to think about it. "Live," he promptly answered.

"Fine. You have a safe in here?"

"A safe?"

"You keep repeating everything I say. It's using up your time," Katz said.

A sound of running feet behind him made the Israeli turn just in time to see a young Chinese approaching, gun in hand, as if to warn the manager of danger. Gaping at the stranger with a submachine gun in his hand, the young man skidded to a halt and raised his pistol.

Too late.

A stream of parabellum manglers slammed him backward onto the painted concrete floor, blood pooling beneath him. It was the last straw for the sex club's manager. He raced around the desk, crawled underneath it with Katzenelenbogen watching him and got the floor safe open in five seconds flat.

Katz didn't know the day's exchange rate, and he didn't have a chance to count the bundled currency as it filled a plastic shopping bag, but there were thousand-guilder notes in there, along with hundreds, fifties and a host of smaller bills.

Not bad.

"Okay," he told his hostage when the safe was empty, "you can go now. Tell your red pole this is only the beginning, right? He's got a migraine coming that will blow his head off."

"Migraine?"

"Never mind," Katz told him, pointing to the exit with his SMG. "You improvise. And move your ass before I change my mind."

The man was running like a track star when he hit the alley, never looking back. He didn't see his adversary follow him outside, turn in the opposite direction from the open door and vanish into darkness with the sack of cash.

IT WOULD HAVE BEEN a relatively simple job to set the place on fire. A thermite canister through any window facing the street would do it, gut the place in no time, but Bolan didn't want to kill the girls or paying customers. He had dropped the hammer on a woman more than once, but each was armed and doing everything within her power to kill him at the time. As for civilian bystanders, he had an ironclad rule against involving them in any action that would cost an innocent's life.

Which meant that he would have to clear the Triad brothel before he burned it down.

Okay.

The getting in was easy. All he had to do was knock and smile at the attractive hostess on the door. She led him to a common room, where women dressed in filmy lingerie or their birthday suits lined up to greet him, offer him a drink, compete for his attention and his cash. A couple of them started screaming when he brought out the Uzi, and Bolan left them to it, waiting for the muscle to appear.

They didn't keep him waiting long.

One of the Triad soldiers was upstairs, his clumping footsteps all the warning Bolan needed, and he was ready for him as his legs came into view before the rest of him. There was a blackjack in his fist, some kind of compromise in weaponry until he checked out the problem, but Bolan shot him anyway, a short burst to his chest that dropped him in a boneless sprawl and spilled him down the stairs.

More screaming, then, and when the next two soldiers came at Bolan, they had pistols in their hands. The gunners started to shoot at their first glimpse of a round-eye with a weapon, wounding two of the girls before the others scattered. Bolan answered with a curse and short precision bursts that stopped the shooters cold. One was stretched out on his back and twitched like a broken robot, while the other went down on his face and didn't move again.

The Executioner checked the injured women, found one barely grazed, more terrified than hurt. The other was bleeding from a flesh wound in her side. When both were on their feet, assisted by their friends and co-workers, he gave them time to fetch clothes from their rooms and make a hasty exit. By the time they started filing out, regarding him with awestruck glances, Bolan had his thermite canisters lined up along the wet bar, waiting for the main event.

When he was satisfied that there was no one left alive inside the brothel, he got down to business, pitched one thermite bomb upstairs and dropped another in the small administrative office, where they also kept a stash of por-

nographic videocassettes on hand for rental to tricks who might require a jump start. Heading for the street, he tossed a third grenade behind the bar and sprayed the ranks of liquor bottles with his Uzi, adding fuel to help the coming flames take hold.

Outside, pedestrians were staring, drawn by sounds of gunfire and the rapid exodus of working girls, but Bolan made no effort to conceal his face. Experience had taught him that the best eyewitnesses were next to useless in emergencies, and most of those on hand were gaping at the upstairs windows, where a cloud of smoke was drifting out to stain the sky.

Nobody tried to stop Bolan and no one followed him as he walked the long block to his waiting rental car. The fire was something tangible, and women—many of them almost nude—were spilling from adjacent houses now as fire alarms began to clamor on the street. It was enough of a diversion that the Executioner could slip away, if not unnoticed, then at least forgotten in the crush.

He thought of Tu Sheng, the target who had dodged him back in London, and decided it was time to try a different angle of attack. Thus far, he had been concentrating on the local Triad and ignoring its political connection with Beijing. But that was all about to change.

The Executioner was seeing Red.

4

The radio told Tu Sheng that it was time for him to run. He didn't like it, but the obvious alternative was tantamount to suicide. If he remained to face his enemies, he would surely die. In Paris he could find another place to hide, regroup and cut his losses, try to start afresh.

The Dragon would be furious, but that couldn't be helped. Ideal reactions in a killing situation seldom matched the choices available in reality. Would it somehow be better for the People's Revolution if Sheng remained in Amsterdam and let himself be slaughtered like an animal?

He didn't need a crystal ball to answer that one. The decision had been made, his bag was packed and he had telephoned ahead to Schipol Airport for his ticket, first-class all the way. It was incumbent on a diplomat to represent his homeland well and generate respect whenever possible.

Before he started to relax, though, Sheng would have to make it to the airport in one piece. That meant departing from his apartment as soon as possible, escaping while the chance remained. He had two escorts from the Triad, one to drive, the other riding shotgun.

It would have to be enough.

He wondered idly whether one of his watchdogs had told Yau that he was bailing out. It hardly mattered now. If either of them tried to stop him, Sheng would use the pistol he had tucked inside his belt. If not, there would be time

enough to ditch it in the men's room at the airport prior to boarding his flight.

Whatever happened, he wasn't about to let himself be killed for nothing in a white man's city far from home. There was a world of difference between a willing sacrifice, in service to the People's Revolution, and a simple waste of life. Sheng had vowed to sacrifice himself if absolutely necessary, but without some order from the Dragon, it would be for him to say when that necessity arose.

This day, he had decided after due consideration, wouldn't be the day.

He made a final sweep of the apartment, making sure that nothing had been left behind to trap him later. Sheng had rented the apartment in another name, with bogus documents supporting that identity, and there would be no comebacks later when his check bounced and the next month's rent was overdue. Landlords didn't trace fingerprints, and his weren't on file with Dutch authorities in any case.

All set, then. He could leave without concern, and if his travels ever brought him back to Holland, Sheng would wear a new identity—perhaps a brand-new face, as well. The surgeons in Beijing were masters at transforming agents of the People's Revolution, thus allowing them to serve repeatedly in areas where they would otherwise have been arrested, even hunted down.

Sheng sent one of his escorts to check the street and smiled at the report that there were no apparent traps in place on Walsteeg. It was beneath his dignity to carry luggage, but he made the sacrifice this time so that his guards could have their gun hands free in case of any unexpected trouble. Only after he was seated in the gray Mercedes-Benz did Sheng relax a bit, beginning to believe that he would make it.

Even so, he spent the drive to Schipol checking fearfully behind them, watching for any indication of a tail. The

driver should have spotted it, but Sheng believed in looking out for number one. He wouldn't trust another with his life, unless he took precautions for himself.

At Schipol he allowed one of the bodyguards to take his bags inside the terminal; the other waited in the car. Sheng didn't thank him, barely nodding at the soldier before the man disappeared in the crowd. He felt a trifle anxious as he dropped his pistol in the men's room trash and covered it with paper towels, but seven minutes later he was safe in the first-class departure lounge.

As safe as he could be in Amsterdam, at any rate.

Sheng bought himself a double whiskey and settled in to wait. He would have time in transit to consider how the Dragon would react to this, his latest getaway.

Meanwhile he was alive.

What more could he expect or hope for in the middle of a war?

BOLAN PARKED his rental two doors down from Sheng's apartment building and walked back. He didn't know exactly what he should expect, but there were no guns on the street, no lookouts visible in upstairs windows to his left or right. If gunners were watching out for Sheng, they knew enough about their job to make a point of keeping out of sight.

With one hand on the Uzi, Bolan mounted concrete steps and entered the apartment building's lobby. To his left mailboxes were arranged in rows, six deep and eight across. The other wall had artwork of a sort, some kind of abstract paintings that were mostly daubs of gaudy color thrown together without seeming rhyme or reason.

Bolan waited for the elevator, stepped inside and punched the button for Sheng's floor, then stepped out again and let the empty car go up without him. He was running when he hit the stairs, ten flights to put him out on the fifth floor, but he was counting on the fact that any sentries would be mo-

mentarily distracted by the elevator. When he reached the fifth-floor service door, he hesitated long enough to catch his breath, then took a firm grip on his SMG and barged into the corridor—to find it empty.

The Executioner felt his stomach knotting as the elevator doors slid shut. The car departed as it had arrived, without a passenger, and Bolan spent another moment waiting, almost hoping for an ambush, something that would tell him he wasn't too late.

Where were the guards? Had Yau abandoned his accomplice from Beijing?

The Executioner moved along the hall with long, swift strides, his weapon covering each door in turn, prepared for anything. Apartment 5D occupied the northeast corner of the floor, the last apartment on his right. As with the other fifth-floor apartments, its door was painted blue.

He wasted no time knocking, but gave the door a solid kick that snapped the lock and carried him across the threshold into darkness. Bolan hit a fighting crouch, dodged to his left, aware that he would make a perfect target with the hallway's light behind him.

Nothing.

Thirty seconds later, knowing he had come too late, he rose and found the light switch, flicked it on and closed the door behind him. How much time? He had no way of knowing whether he had roused the neighbors or if one of them would summon the police, but it wouldn't take long for him to search the place.

He went directly to the master bedroom, checked the closet and the dresser, noting a suspicious dearth of clothes. Sheng had taken everything he owned, from all appearances, the empty drawers and hangers indicating that he wouldn't be returning soon, if ever.

Bolan finished going through the motions—bathroom, kitchen, parlor—just in case, but there was nothing to suggest that Sheng had simply picked this day to start that

overdue vacation he had meant to take for months. It was another bail out, plain and simple. This time, though, he didn't have a fix on where his target might have gone.

There was a notepad by the telephone, some hotel's logo on the top. The pages were blank, as he riffled through, but Bolan's eye picked out the faint impression of handwriting on the topmost sheet of paper. Now, if Sheng had only jotted down the note in English, rather than Chinese...

He checked three kitchen drawers before he found a stubby pencil, long forgotten, hiding underneath a tray of silverware. He lacked an artist's touch, but got the job done, scribbling lightly on the pad until the faint impressions had become white numerals and letters on a darker background: "KLM 2163."

A flight on Royal Dutch Airlines. Going where? Departing when? A phone call to the airport could retrieve those answers, but he couldn't tarry any longer in the empty apartment. The neighbors might be deaf and dumb, but Bolan still had work to do in Amsterdam before he went in search of Tu Sheng.

And there was never any doubt in Bolan's mind that he would follow Sheng.

The agent from Beijing thought he could run and hide, but he was only half-right. Running was the easy part, but he could only run so far.

And there was no safe haven in the world that would protect him from the Executioner.

IT WAS APPROACHING daybreak when McCarter took his place behind Kin Yau's expensive block of condominiums on Oudezijdskolk.

A chill had crept into his bones, but he was ready, psyched up for the raid that was supposed to ring down the curtain on their excursion to the Netherlands. McCarter understood that Bolan had come up empty when he went to find Tu Sheng, but they could always fix that later. At the mo-

ment they were batting cleanup on the 14K, and they weren't finished yet by any means.

Yau was said to own the building, but he occupied only the topmost floor, according to reports from Bolan's contact with the Amsterdam police—one huge apartment for the boss, and two much smaller flats that served as quarters for his private bodyguards. Yau liked his privacy, and there was no way in or out unless you had an invitation.

So they said.

McCarter would have bet that "they" were wrong.

He would have liked to go with Bolan for the rooftop entry, but he understood that someone had to watch the rear, cut off that angle of escape when it hit the fan. With Katz in front, they had their target well and truly boxed, assuming he hadn't flown off to parts unknown with Sheng.

On Bolan's signal from above, the Phoenix Force warriors would move in and close the trap on anyone inside. Ideally they would make a clean sweep of the red pole's private aerie and decapitate the 14K in Amsterdam. Whatever happened with the Triad family after that, it would be someone else's headache.

"I'm in."

The voice was crystal clear, McCarter's tiny earpiece picking up the signal from on high without a trace of interference. Bolan was inside the building, closing on his target, and the time had come for Phoenix Force to do its part.

McCarter went in through the service door and rode the elevator up to the sixth floor, one floor below his target. Elevator access to the top floor took a special key, which he didn't possess, but it was no great strain to use the stairs from the floor.

By the time the elevator stopped, McCarter had his MP-5 K submachine gun out and ready, leading with the stubby weapon as he left the car and hurried to the nearby service door, then the stairs beyond. He took the stairs three at a time, imagined Katz in much the same position at the

far end of the building, closing off the other exit to their enemies.

He stood outside the service access door on the seventh floor and peered through the tiny window that was two glass panes with wire mesh in between. A Chinese sentry wandered past, disappearing in seconds flat.

Patrolling? Going home to sleep? Just killing time?

McCarter checked his watch and saw that he was out of time. There would be no more signals or directions from their leader; they had worked out the plan in advance and knew the moves by heart. McCarter had to move now or stand and watch the whole thing fall apart.

He moved.

The shooter he had glimpsed was opening a door to McCarter's left, about to step inside. He heard the whisper of the service door and turned in that direction, his frown becoming an expression of shocked surprise as he saw death staring back at him.

It was no contest, but the shooter had to try it anyway. He made a jerky grab for hardware and he had to have known that he would never make it. You could give him points for effort, but the brass ring hung impossibly beyond his reach.

McCarter stroked a short burst from his SMG and opened up the gunman's chest. His target staggered, rubber legs collapsing under him, and he went down. The MP-5 K had no silencer, and any notions of a soft approach were banished instantly.

McCarter had known it would come down to this, and he was ready for it. He'd take the open doorway first and see if there was anybody home. If so, the tenants would be scrambling for their weapons now, but there was still a chance to catch them while they were confused, disoriented.

Any edge was preferable to none at all.

He reached the door and ducked inside.

THE GODFATHER of Chinatown was sleeping fitfully when someone grabbed his shoulder, jarring him awake. He came up in a rush, fists clenched and ready to defend himself, before he recognized his bodyguard.

"Ling, what is it?"

"Trouble."

Even as the man spoke, a muffled burst of automatic gunfire ripped the early-morning stillness. Yau leaped out of bed, almost colliding with his soldier, only now discovering the man's pistol ready in his hand.

"How many?"

"I don't know." Ling shrugged as if to emphasize his ignorance.

"The others?"

"I came to wake you first."

"All right. Go find them. Wait! First call Chung Man for help. Tell him to hurry!"

"Yes, sir."

Yau pulled on his dressing gown and fumbled in the top drawer of his nightstand for the pistol he kept hidden there. It was a Walther PPK, small but deadly in the proper hands. Not much against machine guns, granted, but his men had better weapons. They would stand between Yau and his enemies.

If they were still alive.

Yau caught himself before the panic could take root and blossom. He wasn't done yet by any stretch. Gunfire outside the apartment was one thing; he could still defend himself, sit tight until his reinforcements came—or the police, whichever got there first. It made no difference now. He was the victim, and deserving of protection. Any minor firearms violations could be dealt with when the smoke cleared, once his enemies were dead or safely locked in jail.

And it amounted to the same thing in the end. If they lived long enough to be arrested, Yau would find a way to punish them himself, regardless of security precautions.

Such an insult had to be avenged if he intended to preserve his reputation as a ruthless man of power.

Yau cocked the Walther and left the safety off as he turned back in the direction of his living room. There were more sounds of gunfire from the corridor outside his apartment, and he could hear his bodyguard speaking into the telephone, relaying orders. It would take some time for Chung Man to respond, collect his troops and get them on the road, but Yau had had men on standby ever since the trouble began the previous afternoon.

As Yau was entering the living room, a burst of automatic fire ripped through the door of his apartment, bullets slapping into walls and ceiling. He retreated to the bedroom, left his bodyguard to deal with anyone who might come charging through that door. Yau wished there were a fire escape outside his window, but the newer buildings had dispensed with such anachronisms. In the case of an emergency, he could escape by stairs or elevator, maybe leap down to the street below if all else failed. It was a drop of fifty feet or more, and Yau wasn't prepared to take that grim, irrevocable step.

Not yet.

He closed the bedroom door behind him, briefly thought of blocking it with furniture, then decided it would be a foolish risk. A barricade would keep him in, as well as keeping adversaries out. If he was forced to flee in haste, Yau didn't care for the idea of being trapped by obstacles which he himself had set in place.

The firing sounded closer now. He still couldn't be sure exactly who was firing, but it stood to reason that his own men wouldn't use their weapons in the absence of a living, hostile target. If this was some bizarre mistake...

Impossible.

He walked around the king-size bed, then sat on the deep-pile carpeting so that his head and shoulders were the only part of him exposed above the mattress. It wasn't much in

the way of cover, but he knew a mattress would stop bullets fairly well, and Yau would have a clear shot at his enemies as they came through the bedroom door.

If they got that far, it would mean that he was all alone, his soldiers dead or rendered helpless to assist him. It would be the end.

But he could go down fighting, even so.

It was the best way for a man to die.

THE SERVICE STAIRS SEEMED awfully steep to Katz as he was climbing, counting flights and cursing every other step or so. Already winded, and he hadn't even glimpsed the enemy.

He briefly wondered if he was getting too old for fieldwork, then pushed the thought away to concentrate on more-important matters. Like survival, when he reached the seventh floor and the bullets started flying.

He paused on the landing to catch his breath and stiffened as he heard a door slam somewhere overhead. On seven? If so, what did it mean?

Before his mind could come to grips with either question, Katzenelenbogen heard the sharp, staccato sounds of automatic-weapons fire.

He cursed himself aloud and was starting up the next-to-last flight when his ears picked up the sound of hasty footsteps coming down to meet him. Katz was crouching with his right side braced against the metal banister, his Uzi leveled from the hip, as a young Chinese came into view.

Deserting under fire? En route to call for reinforcements? It didn't matter.

The young man had a pistol in his hand, already bringing it to bear on Katz as recognition of an enemy showed in his face. The Israeli beat him to it, squeezing off a burst that stitched the Triad gunner from his waist to his chin, explosive impact lifting him completely off his feet and body-slamming him against the metal stairs. He dropped the shiny automatic and wound up in a huddled sprawl at Katz's feet.

It had been too close for comfort, one of those events no one could ever really plan for in a combat situation. Shaken but unharmed, Katz stepped across the lifeless body and resumed his climb. The sounds of battle echoed all around him in the stairwell, a reminder of his late arrival on the scene that made his ears ring, sparking pain behind one eye.

He had a job to do, and there was nothing to be gained by agonizing over unavoidable delays. He reached the seventh-floor landing, peered out through the tiny window in the service door and saw enough to tell him he was needed on the other side.

From where he stood, two enemies were visible in profile, firing down the hallway to his right, in the direction of some target Katz couldn't see from where he stood. Was it McCarter? Bolan? *Someone* was returning fire, which made his next move doubly perilous, but Katz couldn't stand by and watch the action from the sidelines any longer.

It was time to move.

He shouldered through the service door and caught one of the Triad hardmen turning to investigate the unexpected sound and movement on his flank. Katz stroked the Uzi's trigger, slammed a 4-round burst into his target's rib cage. The shooter staggered, reeling, impact and momentum finishing the turn he had begun with conscious thought. His weapon was a Czech-made Skorpion, and it was spitting death at Katz even as the youthful gunman toppled to the floor.

Katz hit the deck, heard bullets rake the wall above his head, a couple of them spanging off the metal access door. None struck him, and he lay facedown and waited for the storm to pass. Incoming rounds from somewhere down the hall—McCarter's theoretical position—tore into the wallpaper nearby, and Katz saw human targets dodging, weaving, trying to protect themselves.

Three men, goddammit, two of whom had been invisible before he left the shelter of the stairwell.

He came up firing, holding down the Uzi's trigger, sweeping all in front of him. Katz had one chance to get it right, if McCarter didn't shoot him in the meantime by mistake.

It always came to this at last: the killing, one-on-one. It was a soldier's job, the moment he'd prepared for from his first trip to the firing range, in basic training. It was never pleasant—*almost* never, Katz amended silently—but there was no escaping it. Why else, indeed, would there be soldiers in the first place?

Snarling like a cornered animal and firing from the hip, Katz met his enemies and let them have a taste of hell on earth.

THE ENTRY HAD BEEN relatively simple. A service door up on the roof had yielded to his picks, and Bolan scrambled down a short, wall-mounted ladder into darkness. With his feet on solid flooring, he risked a light and found himself inside some kind of service closet, housing brooms, an upright vacuum cleaner, paper towels and cleansers. When he cracked the door an inch, he found himself inside a bedroom, small but amply furnished, with a door that opened on a lighted corridor beyond. The sleeping quarters of a live-in bodyguard, perhaps.

He had the bedroom to himself and moved swiftly toward the open door directly opposite his closet hideaway. There was no time to waste, as the Phoenix Force warriors would be making their move, responding to his signal from the roof. They'd be on their way by now, in fact, and while he couldn't clear the way for their approach, he *could* get on about his business—hunting Kin Yau.

The sprawling suite of rooms was Yau's apartment obviously, but the live-in guard or servant wouldn't sleep adjacent to the master. Bolan spied an intercom beside the bed and pictured Yau calling for his bodyguard in the middle of the night to satisfy some errant whim. The Executioner had

no floor plan to guide him in his search, but he had eyes and ears, which ought to do the trick with any luck at all.

The corridor ran to his left, and Bolan followed it, moving cautiously. He heard a television playing softly somewhere up ahead, and assumed that would be the living room. A guard was on duty, then, to help Yau sleep at night.

The sound of automatic-weapons fire froze Bolan in his tracks. His comrades had arrived outside, and he could now count the time still left to him in seconds.

The television set clicked off. Someone was moving toward him from the direction of the living room. He had a choice to make—reveal himself at once or try to spot his target first—and Bolan chose discretion over zeal. A closet to his right provided ample cover, and he kept the door cracked, saw Yau's bodyguard duck into another bedroom farther down the hall. Two muffled voices spoke Cantonese, then the guard reappeared, moved back in the direction of the living room and the front door.

Yau showed himself a heartbeat later, seemed about to join his bodyguard, when a burst of gunfire stitched his door and changed the red pole's mind. Yau doubled back into his bedroom and slammed the door. Whatever else went down from that point on, it was apparent that the godfather of Chinatown would try to ride it out and let his soldiers take the heat as much as possible.

Yau didn't know the heat was coming for him, even as he huddled in his bedroom, praying for a break.

Emerging from the closet, Bolan moved along the hallway, past Yau's bedroom, toward the parlor. By the time he got there, Yau's bodyguard had gone to join his comrades, fighting to defend their master in the rooms and corridor outside.

So much the better. For the next few moments, anyway, it meant that the Executioner would have the red pole to himself.

He didn't bother checking out the bedroom door. It might be locked or not; in either case Yau would be watching it, most likely armed, and it was probable that he would open fire with everything he had the first time someone touched the doorknob. Bolan kicked the door instead, went through it in a diving shoulder roll and fetched up hard against a heavy antique dresser.

The first shot missed him by at least a yard and gouged plaster from the wall in the corridor outside. Yau cursed in Cantonese and tried again, his second bullet chipping splinters from the ancient chest of drawers. A short burst from the Uzi drove him under cover, crouched behind the king-size bed, and Bolan saw a chance to make his move.

It was a risky proposition, but they couldn't very well trade shots all night across the bed that separated them. Nor could he tag Yau with a burst fired underneath the bed, since it was mounted on some kind of solid platform, adding several inches to its normal height. Royal treatment all the way, and while the setup hadn't been created with defense in mind, it had the same effect in any case.

He palmed a frag grenade and yanked the pin, pushed off with heels against the wall and pitched the bomb as he rolled in closer to the bed. Most of the shrapnel should go up and out—the bed would clearly take its share—and while he wasn't terribly concerned about a shrapnel wound, the blast would still be deafening.

The mattress lifted off, propelled by the concussion of the blast, as if some giant chef were flipping pancakes in Yau's bedroom. Bolan saw it coming and brought his knees to his chest as light was blotted out, the weight descending on him like a body slam. His arms were tangled in the bedding, thrashing hopelessly for precious seconds, while the shrapnel flew around him, scoring plaster, wood and flesh.

He didn't hear Yau die, but the results were obvious as Bolan freed himself from his encumbrance, scrambled clear and eased around the smoking remnants of the bed to find

his prey. The godfather of Chinatown had clearly tried to save himself, retreat from the grenade, since most of his raw shrapnel wounds were in the back and side. Yau's robe, pajamas and the flesh beneath were shredded, blood drenched. Mama Yau wouldn't have recognized him, but the Executioner had no doubts that the corpse before him once had been a ranking member of the 14K.

With ears still ringing, he moved back in the direction of the living room. It was peculiar how the sounds of combat faded, once your eardrums had been dealt a solid blow.

No, it wasn't simply deafness from the blast. Outside, the firing had subsided. Bolan picked out voices, calling back and forth along the corridor, but they spoke English, with familiar accents.

"Coming out!" he warned the Phoenix Force warriors, hoping one or both of them could hear a damn sight better than he could. The risk of friendly fire was ever present in close-quarters combat, and he didn't take it lightly.

"Come ahead," Katz called.

Paris

The easy part was tracing KLM 2163, the flight from Amsterdam to Orly International Airport, just south of Paris. Bolan nailed it with a phone call to the airline's toll-free information number, then made his next call to arrange a hasty charter flight for three beleaguered businessmen who had to make an early-morning confab with potential clients in the advertising industry. The pilot wasn't interested, as long as they paid cash up front.

The best thing about Europe, Bolan thought, was how variety and change stood side by side with ancient history. You couldn't drive ten miles without encountering some landmark from the Middle Ages, Renaissance or Reformation sharing space with high-rise office towers, software factories and new apartment buildings. More to the point, each border crossing introduced new languages and culture, culinary styles and dress codes. In the States a traveler could drive for days on end across vast deserts and rolling plains, and the barns and gas stations and fast-food restaurants all looked the same. In Europe all you had to do was drive around the block to find a change of scene.

But some things never changed.

The Triads' way of doing business, for example. When the Chinese mob put down its roots in Paris, as in every other Western city where the 14K or its competitors were well es-

tablished, it began in Chinatown, spread out from there by stages, forging treaties with the local syndicates when they could not be overcome by force of arms. The Mafia, the Medellín cartel, the Corsican Milieu, the Yakuza—all these and more had made their peace with representatives from Hong Kong and Macao, to keep the drugs and money flowing smoothly into greedy hands.

The Chinese quarter might not be so obvious in Paris as in Amsterdam or London, but it still existed. Above the Parc Monceau, between the Avenue de Villiers and the Boulevard de Corcelles, the Far East had invaded Paris, slowly taking over through the years, until a hapless visitor might be forgiven for suspecting he had been set down in San Francisco or New York by accident. The street signs were in French, but Cantonese was still the major tongue of commerce.

Bolan stood a half block south of Rue Jouffroy, outside the Yang-rou Club, and felt a nagging sense of déjà vu. It was a pain to start from scratch each time Tu Sheng slipped through his fingers, but he had no choice. If nothing else, the unexpected tour of Western Europe was allowing him a chance to shake the 14K in several venues, let the shock waves spread to maximum advantage while his enemies were scrambling to find out what was going on. It brought a smile to Bolan's face, imagining the calls that had to be burning up the lines to Hong Kong and Macao, one echo of disaster following another, weakening the fat, malignant octopus as first one tentacle and then another was destroyed.

No lethal damage was inflicted on the monster yet, but they were making progress. Step by step the 14K was losing ground to Bolan's swift and well-coordinated campaign. He had too much experience to count his chickens yet, but it was still a hopeful sign that he had come this far without a major setback in the field.

Small favors, Bolan thought, and concentrated on his target just across the street. It was too early for the place to

be unlocked; not even janitors would be around at this time of the morning, but he didn't mind. For Bolan's purposes, an empty club would do just fine.

The small athletic bag he carried held five pounds of Semtex plastic explosive, with a twelve-volt battery and detonator he could trigger by remote control. All he had to do was slip inside the club, secure his parcel and retreat a block or so to set it off. No sweat. Round one in Paris would be his, no fuss, no muss.

The Executioner was whistling softly as he crossed the street.

MCCARTER SAW HIS TARGET coming, flanked by goons, emerging from the posh apartment house on Rue de Phalsbourg. Three men were on the sidewalk now, and number four was waiting with the car, a charcoal gray Mercedes-Benz. The car might not be armored, but McCarter didn't want to take the chance.

His mark was Sun Fan, a chief lieutenant in the Triad family led by Toh Lim. While Paris was Lim's seat of government, his influence was also strongly felt in Lyon and Marseilles, where Asian opium was processed into heroin and uncut China white was "stepped on" prior to resale on the streets. Most of the heroin came in from Amsterdam, but Lim had also forged a lucrative alliance with the Medellín cartel, wherein he purchased cocaine by the ton and handled distribution for the whole of France.

That kind of business needed muscle standing by, and Sun Fan had made his reputation as a leg-breaker, assassin and arsonist. He wasn't a large man, but he obviously had a killer attitude.

McCarter crossed the street and came up behind his target, one hand in the pocket of his trench coat wrapped around the MP-5 K submachine gun's pistol grip. No silencer for this job—he would be relying on surprise, audacity and speed to see him through. If anything went wrong,

the Briton understood that the penalty for failure would be death.

A dozen paces separated predator and prey, no more than half that distance left between the three Chinese and their Mercedes-Benz. The driver stayed behind the wheel and kept the engine running. One of Fan's flankers would be handling the doorman's duties this time out.

McCarter's targets were within accepted killing range. He raised the SMG and pointed it from fifteen feet away. There was no need to aim this close, but there was no point taking foolish chances, either. Picking out a point between the left-hand gunner's shoulder blades, McCarter held down the MP-5 K's trigger and swept the stubby man-shredder from left to right, staccato thunder in his ears, brass streaming out of the ejection port to rattle on the pavement.

They went down like puppets with their strings cut, tangling together as they fell. Sun Fan was twitching, but a final 3-round burst relaxed him. Blood ran down the sloping sidewalk toward McCarter, forming crimson streams.

He stepped aside to let it pass.

The driver was emerging now, a pistol in his hand, the car between them. It was too late for his boss, but he couldn't be sure of that, and honor called for him to make the effort.

The Briton fired a short burst from the hip to test the Benz's window glass for bulletproofing, and it shattered instantly, dissolving into pebbles. Satisfied with the result, he held down the trigger and used up the remainder of his magazine to nail the driver where he stood, wrongly believing he was safe.

The man staggered, squeezing off a shot as he went down, but it flew high and wide. He dropped from sight behind the Benz, and McCarter circled far enough around the car to verify a solid hit before he turned his back and put the killing ground behind him. Curtains stirred on both sides of the main residential street, but no one ran outside to challenge

him. Police—or Lim's people—would eventually hear the story of a white man who had pulled the trigger on four Triad soldiers, and the word would get around.

As planned.

The blitz in Paris would require a slightly different angle of attack than Amsterdam, since more-diverse participants were in the game. That made things doubly difficult in some respects, but if they pulled it off, the end result would be more damaging for Triad interests in the city—and in France at large—than if they simply killed Lim and let it go at that.

They had a chance to bring down the house this time, and the opportunity was too good to ignore.

McCarter walked back to his car, climbed in and drove away.

Toward Judgment Day.

TU SHENG WAS DOZING when the phone rang, jarring him awake as if someone had dashed a bucket of cold water in his face. The room was dark, thick curtains drawn against the daylight, and he fumbled for the telephone receiver, nearly dropping it before he got it to his ear.

"Hello?"

Sheng recognized the voice at once. Toh Lim wasn't a man to shout when he was angry; rather, he was prone to speak more softly as his fury escalated toward the detonation point. It didn't please Sheng to realize that Lim was almost whispering.

He sat and listened as the red pole told him what was happening in Paris: four men were executed by a round-eye with an automatic weapon, in full view of several witnesses; there had been a bomb blast at the nightclub where Lim stopped for drinks and dinner several times each week. The godfather of Chinatown had questions for Sheng, concerning London, Amsterdam, the curse Sheng seemed to carry with him as he fled across the continent from faceless enemies. A car had been dispatched to pick him up. He

should be ready when Lim's soldiers rang the bell, so they weren't compelled to wait.

It never crossed Sheng's mind to run away before the gunmen came to fetch him. Bailing out of Amsterdam was one thing, when the tide of battle had already turned against his Triad "friends" and there was nothing he could do to help them on his own. It was a different thing entirely to ignore a summons from the local red pole when he asked for—or, more properly, demanded—information that might save the day in Paris.

Not that Sheng had much to say. He had been fortunate so far in managing to sidestep lethal contact with the unknown enemy. He didn't doubt that those responsible for the attacks in Amsterdam and London were the same men now at work in Paris, but that knowledge wouldn't help Lim protect himself.

Sheng dressed in haste, ignoring the mirror until it was time to brush his hair. His tie was crooked, and he left it that way. Fashion was the least of his concerns.

He thought of reaching out for contact with the Dragon, asking for advice, but finally decided it would be a waste of time. He had to look bad enough already, running for his life while two important segments of their network were reduced to ashes. Still, the Dragon had to realize that Sheng wasn't a gunman. It had never been his job to pull a trigger. He was a negotiator and a fixer, skilled at shoring up alliances between unlikely partners. Much of what the Dragon had accomplished in the European theater of operations would be credited to Sheng.

If he survived.

In realistic terms he knew that no amount of previous success would cover for repeated failures. It was illogical for anyone to blame him for the recent difficulties, but he also understood that logic was in short supply once bullets started flying and the troops began to die.

Sheng *would* be blamed, to some extent, because he had survived the raids in Amsterdam and London, while so many others fell. No matter how he pleaded his case, some would revile him as a coward who had run away to save himself while braver men stood fast and lost their lives. It wouldn't matter that a single man—untrained in combat skills, at that—could make no difference when the Triad's finest troops were going down in flames. It still looked bad for Sheng, and he would have to think of some way to redeem himself.

It would go far in that direction, he decided, if he found a way to help Lim destroy the pesky round-eyes. Sheng had no idea how that could be accomplished, but it seemed the only way for him to come out—how did the Americans express it?—smelling like a rose.

The buzzer sounded, and he went to answer, switching off the lights behind him as he left each room in turn. He took a moment at the door to peer through the peephole, verifying Chinese faces on the other side.

For once the sight of Sheng's fellow countrymen was neither reassuring nor entirely welcome. These men belonged to the Triad, owned body and soul by Lim. At a word from their master, they would dismember Sheng and drop him in the Seine to feed the fish.

It wasn't likely that the godfather of Chinatown would kill him, risk the Dragon's wrath, but Sheng couldn't absolutely rule it out. If his survival seemed to threaten Lim, his family or the 14K at large, Sheng had no doubt that loyalty to the Triad and self-preservation would prevail.

His work would all have been for nothing, then.

More to the point, he would be dead and gone.

Sheng's hands were trembling as he opened up the dead bolt and turned the knob, but he was smiling as he greeted Lim's warriors. Three cold faces stared at him, jackets open so that they could reach their weapons.

"I'm ready," Sheng informed them. "Shall we go?"

KATZ FOUND HIS TARGETS sitting down to breakfast in a restaurant on Rue Cardinet. There were eight of them, all *cho-hai*—sharks—who handled muscle work in Paris and environs for the 14K. These were the men who went to see you if you stiffed the family on loan payments or your merchant's tribute for the month was running late. They were extortionists by trade and brutes by inclination, savages in any language.

The Israeli crossed the busy street, moved swiftly down an alley on the east side of the restaurant and went in from the back. The kitchen smells made his stomach growl, reminding him that he had eaten nothing since a sandwich on the charter flight from Amsterdam.

There would be enough time later to take care of that, if he got through the next few moments safe and sound.

He kept the Uzi submachine gun hidden underneath his raincoat as he passed the bustling kitchen, glancing in at the workers in their snow-white jackets. They were spotless to a man, and too absorbed in work to pay him any mind. A couple of them glanced at Katzenelenbogen, recognized a stranger in their midst and quickly turned away.

It took all kinds, he thought, and Katz could only guess what kind of hard-eyed customers passed through a Triad hangout in the course of any given week. Colombians, Corsicans, Sicilians, an American or two, some would-be mobster in from London to negotiate a deal for China white. The kitchen help, he calculated, wouldn't be surprised by much of anything.

At least, until the guns went off.

Once he was past the kitchen, Katz had a straight shot to the dining room. It wasn't crowded at this hour. In fact, aside from Katz's targets and their waiter, there was no one in the place. That made it easier, at least in theory, since he wouldn't have to think about civilians blundering across his line of fire.

He crossed the open dining room, no hesitation now, his left hand wrapped around the Uzi's pistol grip, the metal claw that was his right hand ready to support the weapon when he opened fire. Another fifteen paces, and the sharks hadn't seen him, yet. The waiter glanced toward Katz, frowning slightly, and seemed about to speak before the scowl on Katz's grim face changed his mind. The young man turned away and started to walk toward the kitchen as if his life depended on it.

Perfect.

Now he had the sharks all to himself.

By the time they saw death coming, Katz was twenty feet away, the Uzi's short, unlovely muzzle sliding out from underneath his coat. He had the weapon cocked, its safety off, before he ever stepped inside the Chinese restaurant, so there was nothing to delay him now.

The gunner farthest from him, at the table's head, was rising, pointing, calling out a warning to his friends in Cantonese. The other seven heads were swiveling to face Katz as he opened fire.

The Uzi's racket was hellacious in the quiet dining room. He swept the far side of the table first, because the gunmen there were facing him as he approached and therefore stood a better chance of returning his fire. Three soldiers tried desperately to rise and reach their weapons as a storm of parabellum manglers punched them over backward, sprawling in their high-backed chairs.

The leader, seated at the table's head, had one hand in his jacket and was lurching to his feet when Katz shot him in the chest. It was a short burst but it did the trick, dumping the shark onto the floor in a boneless sprawl.

Four down and four to go.

Katz kept on firing, sweeping the near side of the table, where a couple of the Triad hardmen had been startled into immobility. They couldn't seem to move, and the Israeli

helped them, blasting both men from their chairs and sending them crashing to the blood-streaked floor.

The last two sharks were on their feet now, weapons in their hands. One fired a wild shot at his round-eyed adversary and received a disemboweling burst in answer to his effort. Number eight, the last survivor, saw a chance to run and took it, sprinting toward the kitchen, but he never made it. Katz used the last rounds in his magazine to drop the runner on his face and nail him there.

Reloading on the move, Katz cautiously retraced his steps and checked out the kitchen, where a pall of utter silence had replaced the normal clatter. He left the staff to take whatever steps they thought appropriate. It made no difference to him if they reached out for the police or Toh Lim. In either case, the red pole would be briefed on what had happened soon enough.

And that was what they wanted, after all. A little extra seasoning tossed in the pot as it began to boil. Somebody would be getting scalded soon, or Katz was very much mistaken.

THE TWO YOUNG TRIAD gunners saw it coming, but their inexperience was such that neither of them knew exactly what to do when death came calling. Both fumbled underneath their stylish jackets for their pistols, but it was too late. When you were covered going in, a weapon cocked and pointed at your face with no diversion handy, there was nothing much to do but pray.

The Beretta spit two silenced rounds at point-blank range. The lookouts never had a chance, but Bolan felt no sympathy for men who chose to make a living from the misery of others. They were voluntary players in a lethal game, and they had lost.

Stepping over crumpled bodies, Bolan tried the back door of Yuan-lin Club and found it wasn't locked. Why should it be, with two brave soldiers standing watch?

He stepped inside and closed the door behind him, listening for any sound that would betray another human presence in the club. The gambling wouldn't start before eleven, maybe twelve o'clock, but he could still hear voices, muffled by an intervening wall somewhere ahead of him. He homed in on the sound, replaced the Beretta in its armpit rig and swung his Uzi from under cover as he closed the distance to his prey.

The club was yet another night spot owned by Lim and company, a combination hangout for the mob and business enterprise designed to separate Chinese civilians from their hard-earned money at the gaming tables. Since there were no customers this early, Bolan would assume the sounds he overheard were made by members of the Triad management.

A door stood open on his left, six paces farther down the corridor. He took his time, aware that some pedestrian might find the stiffs outside at any time, but still less concerned with an alarm than with the consequence of rushing when he had his targets cornered but their strength was unknown.

He risked a peek around the doorjamb, counted four men in the office and decided it was time to introduce himself. The oldest of the four was seated at a desk with ledgers open on the blotter, a compact adding machine replacing the traditional abacus. His three companions ringed the desk and listened to his every word, intent on following the point he sought to make... until the desk man lost his voice and sat back with a gasp, eyes fixed on Bolan and the submachine gun in his hands.

It took a heartbeat for the other three to register the source of his confusion, then they swung around to face the round-eyed stranger in the doorway. Looking at a clear-cut choice of do or die, they tried to *do,* but they were facing even worse odds than their late, unlucky friends out back.

The Uzi stuttered and dropped them in their tracks, one dying soldier slumping back against a nearby filing cabinet, raking coffee cups and magazines from the top as he reached out for some support and missed it, finally sprawling on his face.

The man behind the desk was speechless, staring down the Uzi's muzzle, waiting for his turn to die.

"Speak English?" Bolan asked him.

"Yes."

"May I assume you want to live?"

"What must I do?"

"I have a message for Toh Lim. You pass it on, I pass you by. Fair trade."

"What message?"

"Tell him it's the end. He's out of time. Too many debts are overdue, and I'm collecting. Have you got that?"

"Is the end. No time. Debts coming due."

"That's close enough." Bolan waited for another moment, staring at the man behind the desk, then said, "Are you still here?"

The guy was quick for someone of his age and girth—a senior track star passing Bolan in the home stretch, making for the finish line.

Another seed of discord, sown on fertile ground.

He left a thermite canister behind him in the office, then cleared the club before it started spewing white-hot coals. A Viking funeral might not be appropriate for Chinese gangsters, but it was the best he had to offer.

There would be more funerals coming soon, he thought. Enough to go around for all concerned.

6

It seemed a long walk from the car to Toh Lim's office. Tu Sheng was sweating through his white dress shirt before his escorts brought him to the door marked Private, on the sixth floor of an office building one block south of Avenue de Villiers. One of the hardmen, apparently the leader, knocked and slipped inside, while Sheng and two stern-faced companions lingered in the hallway, waiting for permission to enter.

The minutes dragged like hours, with Sheng determined not to let nerves make him fidget. He wasn't some schoolboy called before the headmaster for cutting up in class. The problems Lim faced weren't Sheng's fault, and he would *not* feel guilty for the fact that he was still alive.

So far.

Sheng knew there was a chance, however slim, that he wouldn't survive his meeting with Lim. For all of his soft-spoken charm, the red pole was a man notorious for both his rages and the vengeance wreaked upon his enemies. Sheng knew a few of the unpleasant stories, and he had no wish to be another piece of Lim's grisly reputation.

The leader of the pickup team returned, a curt nod urging Sheng into the office. None of them accompanied him, which was small relief as the door closed behind him, leaving him alone with Lim.

The red pole sat behind a massive desk of hand-carved ebony. He didn't rise in greeting, didn't smile, but waved a

pale hand toward the solitary straight-backed chair that stood before his desk. Sheng crossed the room, sat and waited for the grilling to commence.

"How are you, Sheng?" Lim's voice was soft, low pitched as always. Intimate.

"I'm well," Sheng replied, hoping it was the correct response.

"You have no injuries to show for the events in Amsterdam and London, then?"

Sheng saw the trap and tried to edge around it. "I was fortunate."

"Indeed. A number of my brothers did not share your luck."

"I understand that."

"And do you understand the cause of all this trouble, Sheng? What is your explanation for these treacherous attacks?"

"I have no explanation, Toh."

"Your function, as I understand it, is to harmonize our operations with Beijing and to guarantee that everything runs smoothly. Yes?"

"I do my best. There are no guarantees in life."

"So, you admit to failure, then?"

"I willingly admit these raids against the 14K have come as a surprise—to you, as well, I think."

"It was my understanding that our dealings with the Dragon were supposed to make things better for my family, not get my soldiers killed."

"You think these incidents relate in some way to the Dragon?"

"What am I to think?" Lim asked. "Your counterpart in the United States was killed last week, if I am not mistaken."

"Luk Pang. You are correct," Sheng said.

"And you believe it was a mere coincidence?"

"I have no way of knowing that."

"Am I supposed to be impressed by ignorance?"

Sheng hesitated for a moment, gathering his nerve before he answered. "I want this business settled, just as you do. I do not enjoy being hunted like an animal through half of Europe."

"So, you think these round-eyes *are* pursuing you?"

"I didn't say that. Clearly I have no way to determine who they are or what they want."

"But you continue running from them, all the same. Or should I say you keep on leading them to other targets."

Lim had dropped his voice to something in the nature of a whisper now. Sheng recognized the danger sign, deciding that his best defense was frank defiance.

"If you think I have betrayed you, call your soldiers. Better yet, inform the Dragon of your thoughts. You are familiar, I believe, with his response to traitors."

"I have made no accusations," Lim replied, "but you'll admit the circumstances are . . . peculiar."

"As you say."

"Perhaps it would be wise if you stayed here and let my men watch over you until this matter is resolved."

Sheng felt his stomach rolling, but he couldn't very well refuse the offer without driving Lim to some more drastic act.

"I would be happy to accept your hospitality," he said.

"It's settled, then." The red pole keyed his intercom; Sheng heard the door swing open at his back. "For both our sakes," Lim said, "I hope this trouble will be settled soon."

IT HAD BEGUN as yet another ordinary day, with nothing to commend it, but the morning call had changed all that. Marcel Bouchet wasn't sure what to make of his new orders, but he would do as he was told—up to a point. The Sûreté didn't encourage great initiative among its officers, but he wasn't a slave. Sometimes it was convenient to ignore the book and take things as they came.

Bouchet could only hope the Triads were involved somehow, and that he would obtain new information to help him in his five-year effort to defeat the Chinese syndicate in France. Bouchet wasn't alone in that pursuit, but he still felt that way sometimes. Their progress had been next to nonexistent, and it sickened him to watch Toh Lim expand his rotten empire while the law stood helpless to prevent him.

Bouchet knew there was *something* going on in Paris. That much was apparent from the several violent incidents reported in the past three hours. Triad property or personnel had been on the receiving end in every case, and Bouchet would have been dishonest with himself if he pretended that he wasn't pleased to see the Chinese gangsters squirming for a change.

The heat would do them good, and if it drove them out of Paris altogether, well, sometimes the end *did* justify the means.

The meeting had been set by one of his superiors, with no warning to Bouchet until the order was delivered at his desk by telephone. Proceed to a specific sidewalk café on the Avenue de Champs-Elysées. The man he was supposed to meet—an American called Mike Belasko—hadn't been described. It would be *his* responsibility to find Bouchet, identify himself and take it on from there. The purpose of the meeting was obscure.

He'd been told to listen, hear what Belasko had to say.

About Toh Lim? Could the Americans be interested in Lim's activities somehow? It seemed improbable, unless the red pole was expanding his activities beyond their normal sphere. In that case, anything was possible.

Bouchet watched out for traffic as he passed the Eiffel Tower and crossed the Seine. Most Parisian drivers handled their vehicles as if they were disciples of the kamikaze pilots in the Second World War. It almost seemed to be a point of pride for them to blow their horns at someone every hundred meters, give or take, and near-miss accidents were

like a test of mettle, one more way for men and women to escape their humdrum lives and snatch a moment of adventure from the rat race.

Bouchet knew the feeling—the frustration that came with going nowhere fast, as the Americans would say—but he had enough danger in his life already without seeking more on the road as a form of diversion.

Across the river twenty minutes of dodging his fellow countrymen brought him to a public parking lot, a long block from the street café where he would find the mysterious Yank.

Or maybe not.

It seemed unlikely to Bouchet that this would be a hoax, but stranger things had happened. He even considered the possibility of a trap, but that seemed too improbable to be taken seriously. The Triads could reach out for him at any time, if that was their desire, and while Bouchet didn't always enjoy the best relationship with his superiors, it seemed preposterous that they would join a plot to have him killed.

Still, he was grateful for the pistol in his pocket as he parked the Citroën and walked to the café, due east. He found a table, as instructed, sat and ordered wine. It was too early for a meal, but there was always room for alcohol.

A shadow fell across the wrought-iron table as he sat and waited for his wine. Bouchet glanced up to meet the tall man's eyes.

"Bouchet?"

The agent nodded cautiously.

"I'm Mike Belasko," the American informed him, thrusting out a hand. "It's good to meet you."

"TELL ME MORE about the Triads and the Corsicans," Bolan said, after they had both been served: wine for Bouchet and coffee for himself.

The sandy-haired French officer sat back and scratched his chin reflectively before he spoke. "They tolerate each

other, yes? It is a marriage of convenience, you would say. The Union Corse—or Corsican Milieu, if you prefer—has been our Mafia in France as long as anybody can remember. Following the Second World War, your CIA hired Corsicans to help disrupt the Communists in France. They're not concerned with politics, per se, unless it has some impact on their earning power. How ironic that they should cooperate with the Chinese today and help the Communists instead of fighting them."

"Times change," Bolan said.

"So they do." Bouchet took time to sip his wine before continuing. "Along with smuggling and assorted other crimes, the Corsicans have dominated heroin in France for many years. Your so-called French Connection, in the 1960s, was a deal between the Corsican Milieu and mafiosi in New York. Traditionally they've imported opium from Turkey and refined it in Marseilles, for sale in France and distribution overseas. More recently, with some assistance from the Triads, they've begun to deal in Asian heroin, as well. More irony—a fair percentage of the drugs refined in France these days is shipped to South America as payment for cocaine. The men from Medellín and Cali have no distribution network here, so they have struck a bargain with the home team, as you say."

"Where does the money go?" Bolan asked.

"Oh, we have our share of laundries here, Monsieur Belasko. To the south, in the Basque provinces, it's known that the Colombians and Triads laundered some one and a half billion francs last year. That's roughly one-third of a billion U.S. dollars, I believe. We shut the operations down whenever possible, of course, but still...it's difficult to outlaw commerce altogether, no?"

"I see your point."

"There are legitimate investments, too. Some forty kilometers from Paris, on the Seine, the Triads own three hundred acres of commercial property. They've built two luxury

hotels, together with a first-class shopping center. There is, of course, no law against improving the economy, creating jobs and so forth."

"So, your hands are tied?"

"Not quite. The drugs are still illegal, and we make arrests, send various conspirators to prison. As in your country, however, those on top take care to insulate themselves from what goes on below. We catch the smaller fish, but sharks avoid the net."

"I take it that you're following the link between the Triads and Beijing," Bolan said.

"It has come to our attention," Bouchet replied, "but the options are limited. Some Chinese visitors have diplomatic immunity, and all are welcome to speak with their countrymen living in France. It is impossible for us to watch each Chinese in Paris, much less in the country."

"Do you recognize the name Tu Sheng?"

Bouchet put on a narrow smile. "That one!" he said. "We watch *him* when we can, but he is skilled at giving us the slip, as you would say. We know about his meetings with Toh Lim and other Triads, but there is no crime in talking."

"That depends on what they talk about," Bolan said.

"True enough, but Lim has learned to take precautions when it comes to—shall we say?—eavesdropping. He retains a small but expert team of security specialists to watch over his home and office, his telephones and vehicles. They've frankly managed to defeat our best equipment for the past three years at least."

"Your problem," Bolan said, "is that you have to make a case in court."

Bouchet responded with a weary shrug. "Of course. Our system is a trifle different from yours, I think. Defendants are required to prove their innocence, instead of simply standing mute and letting us do all the work, but we must still have solid evidence."

"Suppose there was another way to go?"

"And which way would that be?" Bouchet inquired.

"A more direct approach, let's say."

The Frenchman almost smiled, but caught himself and took another sip of wine instead. "You mean a frame-up? Manufactured evidence?"

"No, I was thinking more of straight elimination."

"Ah." The silence hung between them for a moment while Bouchet considered that. "I take it that you do not represent the FBI."

"Not even close."

"Three different letters come to mind."

"Strike two. I don't like working for the Company," Bolan said.

"Would this have anything to do with the events that have transpired since breakfast?" Bouchet asked.

"It would."

"You seem to have a fair start on the problem, as it is. Why would you risk yourself, approaching someone from the Sûreté?"

"I need your help," the Executioner replied. "Your people know the Corsicans and local Triads inside out. Who better, for a target spotter, than someone who spends his whole life studying the enemy?"

"I'm not sure what to make of this," Bouchet replied.

"You mean the fact that your superiors arranged the meeting?"

"For a start."

"Consider it a trend toward international cooperation on solution of a common threat. We could refer it to the diplomats, I guess, but I'd prefer to get a handle on the problem in this century," Bolan said. "How about yourself?"

"You tempt me," Bouchet told him, "but I've been trained to shun temptation in my line of work."

"No strings attached. No one's asking you to pull a trigger, and they never will."

"What, then?"

"The benefit of your experience. Addresses, names, connections. Like a shopping list."

The Frenchman laughed out loud at that, and took another sip of wine before he answered.

"Very well," he said. "We'll have an early Christmas, then. I think I'll treat myself."

Macao

THE DRAGON LIT a cigarette, inhaled and blew smoke from his nostrils, sitting with his eyes closed in the dark. It helped to put his thoughts in order when he stood apart from other men and blocked their shrill, discordant voices from his mind. Most times a little solitude was all he needed to resolve a problem, come up with an answer to some question that bedeviled him.

But not this time.

He had been chasing shadows for a week now, watching as his network was dismantled piece by crucial piece. Five Triad families had been shattered, and a sixth—in Paris—was already reeling from the first resounding blows of what appeared to be another carbon-copy blitzkrieg. Scores of Triad soldiers had been killed, his own chief representative in North America was dead and Tu Sheng was scampering around the European continent like some demented rodent with a starving cat close on his tail.

So far, for all the bloodshed, Cheung Kuo was still no closer to identifying his opponents than he had been on day one.

No, that wasn't entirely true. The Dragon knew that they were round-eyes, almost certainly American, because the trouble had originated in the States. Beyond those basic facts, however, he was at a loss for solid battlefield intelligence. His contacts in the British secret service had reached out to counterparts at Langley, hoping for some kind of

lead, but they had come back empty-handed. If the CIA was sponsoring these raids against his network, they were covering the secret well. No leaks to friendly forces overseas or to police in the United States.

That didn't rule out Company involvement. They were *supposed* to be adept at keeping secrets, after all, though harsh reality was often very different. In normal practice it was Kuo's experience that secrets had a way of leaking out, and great, important secrets frequently sprung massive leaks. By now some hint of what was happening should logically have made the rounds, providing Langley was involved.

And if the CIA was innocent, then who was left? What suspects were available?

Kuo wasn't naive enough to think himself aware of every secret agency or group controlled from Washington. Americans kept up a kind of love affair with their policemen—put them on TV, romanticized their exploits in the cinema and novels. That included secret agents, who were commonly distorted out of all resemblance to reality in media reports and fiction. It would come as a distinct surprise, in fact, if there weren't at least a dozen secret agencies the Dragon didn't know about.

Was one of them assigned to track him down, destroy the network he had worked so long and hard to build? If so, how could he counteract the progress that his enemies had made so far?

The Triads were supposed to be professionals who looked out for themselves. Indeed, that had been the main attraction in seducing them to help him spread the People's Revolution in the West. Their worldwide network was extensive and sophisticated, interlocking with at least a dozen other criminal fraternities from Tokyo to Moscow, Sicily to the United States and South America. The 14K was absolutely ruthless with its enemies, well-known for settling its debts in

blood. The very name was feared wherever Chinese immigrants had put down roots in the New World.

How, then, had five red pole enforcers and their private armies come to grief when they were fighting a defensive battle on familiar ground? Why were police in Holland, England, Canada and the United States unable to suggest a culprit in the string of organized attacks?

The Dragon took a last drag on his cigarette, found the ashtray by touch and stubbed out the butt. His eyes opened on darkness, except for a faint seam of light where the drapery failed to meet perfectly and the glow from a streetlight bled through. He focused on that light, as if it held some revelation for him and would help him find his way.

Tu Sheng had managed to survive thus far, where other men—including Luk Pang—had miserably failed. A part of that success, the Dragon knew, was simple cowardice. Sheng ran away before the enemy got close enough to touch him. Even so, he had escaped from London, then from Amsterdam, and he was still alive in Paris, unless something had befallen him within the past two hours. Was there something he had learned about the enemy, some piece of vital information that he might not even recognize as critical?

It would be worth interrogating Sheng to find out what he knew, but that could be a problem at the present time. Toh Lim had taken Sheng into "protective custody," a thinly veiled captivity that struck the Dragon as an insult to his own integrity. Still, he could understand the red pole's thinking, recognized the fear Lim had to be feeling, even though the man couldn't admit it to himself.

So questioning Sheng would have to wait.

And in the meantime Kuo would have to seek enlightenment in other quarters, learn the names and motives of his round-eyed enemies before it was too late.

The Dragon reached out for his cigarettes and lighter in the darkness.

He was swiftly running out of time.

Paris

TOH LIM WAS FOND of saying that the secret to success was perseverance. He outlasted enemies who seemed at first to have more men, more energy, more zeal, and in the long run they went down before him in defeat. Of course, the fact that he was absolutely ruthless, took no prisoners, also contributed to his success and reputation. In a quarter century of service to the 14K, Lim had ordered, supervised or personally executed some 350 murders; half again as many victims had been killed or maimed in bombings, drive-by shootings and the like while simply passing by or loitering about the scene where one of Lim's intended targets had been marked to die.

All that was business, though, and the attacks he had suffered through the morning had a different feeling to them. They seemed personal somehow, as if an enemy Lim couldn't recall had surfaced from his past, intent on destroying everything that Lim had worked for through the years.

It couldn't be allowed. His very life and reputation were at stake in Paris. If he failed to find his adversaries and destroy them, it would be a death blow for his credibility among his brothers of the 14K. His hill chief in Hong Kong would be entirely justified in picking out another red pole to command the troops in France—assuming any troops survived.

Lim wouldn't permit himself to be humiliated further. Chinatown was *his* preserve, and no round-eye could hope to beat him in the territory he had cultivated so assiduously for so long. His enemies were on a lucky streak, perhaps, but it would break and leave them stranded if they pushed their luck too far.

In fact, Lim told himself, they should be running out of luck already. Every eye in Chinatown was on alert for white men who were obviously foreigners, behaving in unusual

ways. Lim's network hadn't failed him in the past, and he had no good reason to believe that it would fail him now.

But he had seen enough of treachery and back-stabbing, participated in enough of it himself, to know that anything was possible when greed, self-interest and a craving for revenge combined. It was conceivable that someone in his own ranks could betray Lim in hopes of moving up the ladder once he fell. He took whatever steps he could to guard against a traitor in the family, but there was no way to eliminate the risk entirely, not as long as he was forced to work with human beings.

But if all else failed, Lim made his mind up that he wouldn't go without a fight. The sketchy details he received from London, Amsterdam and the United States left much to the imagination where the downfall of his brother red poles was concerned. Lim had no way of knowing whether they were negligent or if their enemies had overwhelmed them with technology and numbers. Lim had seen their work already, and he knew that they were skilled assassins, but he wasn't one to duck and hide from strangers in his own backyard.

If this was war—and so it seemed to be—Lim was prepared to make the streets of Chinatown run red with blood. His businesses would suffer, but no more than if he stood aside and let the round-eyes run amok in Paris, unopposed. At least this way Lim's fearsome reputation would remain intact. The stories carried back to Hong Kong and his hill chief would describe a warrior fighting for his life, not some weak sister hiding in the dark and waiting for the storm to pass.

Lim drained his whiskey glass and reached out for the telephone. He had an army to command, and there was no more time to waste.

The black woolen ski mask was a trifle scratchy on his skin, but Bolan had more-pressing problems at the moment than the mild discomfort of a hastily contrived disguise. He was about to step inside the lion's den, and it was very possible that step could be his last.

In that respect, at least, the mask was critical. His targets this time weren't Chinese, and he was bent on making them believe that *he* might be, if not a Triad soldier, then at least some mercenary hired by Toh Lim to do a dirty, underhanded job.

His height and build were wrong for a Chinese, but Bolan was a master of "role camouflage." He was aware that persons caught up in surprise emergencies most often saw what they expected—or what they were urged—to see. The Corsicans were famous for their paranoia, and it served them well. His conversation with Marcel Bouchet had driven home the point that there was no love lost between the Triads and the Corsican Milieu. There had been blood spilled when the Chinese gangsters first invaded Paris and Marseilles, and the wounds, masked by time, had never truly healed.

And with a little help, the Executioner was confident that he could rip the scabs right off, remind those former enemies that all they had in common were the profits from a business based on treachery and greed.

His target was a Turkish bath off Boulevard du Port-Royal, where heavies from the Corsican Milieu hung out, killed time and generally did nothing much at all, luxuriating in the role of men who weren't required to hold a steady job because the money came to them. The Corsicans were known as brutal killers—French equivalents of the Sicilian Mafia or Medellín cartels—but they were also businessmen, which meant that they weren't out stalking victims on a daily basis. Years of getting rich and fat from heroin, with minimal effective opposition from the law or rival syndicates, had slowed them a little.

Bolan hoped so, anyway.

He went in through the back and smelled sweat and steam before the door had even closed behind him. His marks were rich men, sweating off the hangovers and heavy meals they took for granted, laughing, telling dirty jokes, pretending they were still the lean, mean youths who fought their way up from the gutters of Marseilles, where *flics* would crack your skull with nightsticks for the fun of it and rival gangs would gut you like a fish to steal the spare change in your pockets.

These days they were so secure and comfortable that they didn't even post a lookout when they dropped their trousers and retired to catch some steam. These men were proud that they had no surviving enemies. If the police were coming, for whatever reason, they would more than likely telephone ahead. That's what the weekly bribes were for.

He checked the locker room and found it empty, so kept on going, starting to perspire inside his woolen mask before he reached the steam room proper. Visibility was poor inside there, and swarthy faces turned in his direction, someone calling out in French for him to close the door. No one but mobsters were welcome in this private club, which made it easy for him. He brought out the Uzi, muzzle-flashes eerily reflected by the drifting clouds of steam.

He swept the room from left to right and back again, saw naked bodies sprawling, some in better shape than others, all of them in desperate trouble now. He counted seven men, without a gun among them, and left them sprawling on the steam-slick tile or draped on wooden benches ranged about the walls. Blood mingled with the sweat and condensation, swirling toward a central drain.

Emerging from the steam room, Bolan met a younger man, still dressed, attracted by the sudden noise. The choice was made on instinct. Bolan lashed out to club him with the Uzi's smoking muzzle, rather than immediately killing him. The death card from an *I Ching* deck replaced his pistol in its shoulder holster when the Executioner relieved him of his gun.

It wasn't much in terms of evidence—but, then again, the Corsicans were quick to judge, notoriously flexible when it came down to rules of evidence.

And Bolan wasn't finished with them yet.

THE TRICK, McCarter realized, was *missing* in the heat of battle, when your every instinct sought to send the bullets in on target, leave your adversary stretched out in a pool of blood and make sure that he would never trouble you again. Restraint was seldom cultivated as a virtue of the frontline combat soldier, but it made an interesting change.

So he would do his very best to drop the piglets in their tracks but let the boar survive.

You couldn't be too subtle with the Corsicans. McCarter's chosen weapon for this outing was the Chinese Type 68 assault rifle, their shameless knockoff of the Russian SKS, chambered in 7.62 mm NATO with a 30-round box magazine and a six-power telescopic sight for accuracy. He didn't want to spray the street, but it was good to have some firepower behind him when he put the ball in play.

His rooftop perch on Boulevard Bourdon gave McCarter a clear shot for almost a hundred yards in each direction,

north and south, but his target zone lay directly beneath him. No trick shots would be required for this mission if his adversaries played it straight and went about their daily business in a normal fashion.

And, McCarter thought, why shouldn't they? So far, the violence shaking Paris had been limited to Chinese targets, members of the 14K. If anything, it stood to reason that the Corsicans—not fond of foreigners in general at the best of times, or Chinese in particular—would be amused by any mishaps that befell the Triads. There was no good reason for the French mobsters to suspect that they were next.

Not yet.

McCarter's target was a Corsican named Leon Heuse, who was second-in-command of the French syndicate in Paris, answering directly to the boss of bosses, one François Dupin. In everyday affairs Heuse called the shots for distribution of narcotics, squeezing money from the labor unions, some illegal gambling—all the things, in short, that midrank mafiosi handled in the States. Suspected in at least two dozen murders, he had served eleven months for manslaughter in 1970 before a sympathetic judge "reviewed" the evidence and let him walk. It had been easy street since then, aside from some tense moments with the Triads when they first invaded France. All that was history these days, and Heuse had settled down to making money, saving stories of his gory glory days for nights out with the boys.

McCarter checked his watch, saw Heuse was running late and was about to curse his luck when a Mercedes four-door sedan rolled in from the south and double-parked in front of the apartment building opposite. A moment later his target left the building's lobby and walked onto the sidewalk. Two hardmen preceded their boss, two more bringing up the rear.

It would have been a simple thing to drop Heuse before he reached the Benz, but that wasn't the plan. Eliminating Corsicans was no great challenge, but it took a bit more ef-

fort to provoke them into waging war against their Chinese "allies" in the 14K.

McCarter froze a target in the cross hairs of his scope, a young man with a pale scar on his swarthy cheek. He wasn't smiling but he seemed relaxed. Another day, another boring job.

The boredom ended with a hollowpoint projectile ripping through his forehead, flattening on impact, taking out a fist-size chunk of skull in back and spattering the young man's brains across the sidewalk. By the time they heard the shot, McCarter had another human target in his sights, already taking up the trigger slack.

His second mark was turning toward the dead man stretched out on the pavement, blinking at a glimpse of the impossible, a part of him no doubt aware that he should already be covering his boss.

Too late.

The bullet found him well before the young man made his move, a hit dead center in the chest that rocked him backward on his heels and took him down. McCarter tracked on, his view a blur until the telescopic sight picked out another Corsican and locked in on his face.

The two survivors were intent on shoving Heuse into the car, where he would have at least a minimum of cover from the enemy they couldn't see. McCarter chose the man on Heuse's left and shot him in the neck, a red mist covering the boss's face before he scrambled out of sight inside the Benz.

And that left one.

McCarter could have let him slide, but there was something in him that rebelled at leaving work half-done. The soldier was about to follow Heuse into the vehicle, when yet another shot rang out, and he was catapulted backward, spinning like a dervish as he fell.

The Phoenix Force warrior used up half a dozen rounds on the Mercedes as it powered out of there. He didn't try to

nail the driver, but was content with chipping paint and flattening one tire so that the Benz was forced to limp as it retreated from the ambush scene.

He left the Chinese rifle where it could be found as soon as witnesses or basic calculations led investigators to his roost. In case they missed the point, he palmed the death card from an *I Ching* tarot deck and curled it with his fingers so that it would fit inside the rifle's trigger guard.

It was a whole new game in Paris now, and things would soon be heating up. McCarter caught himself about to break out whistling as he reached the service stairs, and settled for a silent smile.

They weren't done yet, not by any means.

But they were getting there.

FRANÇOIS DUPIN SAT QUIETLY and listened for a second time as Leon Heuse described the ambush. He was soaking up the details, few as there might be, and correlating them with the police report he had received by telephone five minutes earlier.

The police had found a rifle and some kind of playing card, apparently left by the sniper as a message to his enemies. The weapon and the card were both Chinese.

What did it mean?

Dupin was clear on what it *seemed* to mean, but life had taught him that appearances were frequently deceptive. Everybody lied; he knew that from experience. The standard rule of thumb in Dupin's business was to trust no one unless you had complete and absolute control of a specific individual, the power of life and death. Dupin enjoyed that power over his subordinates, and even they were known to try to deceive him from time to time. As for the world at large...

A Chinese rifle. Chinese military-surplus ammunition. And a Chinese playing card.

Could Toh Lim really be that foolish? If he meant to break their treaty, start an all-out shooting war, would he bend over backward to announce the fact and point a guilty finger at himself?

Perhaps.

The godfather of Chinatown was well-known for his arrogance, a trait François Dupin could well appreciate, because he shared it to a large degree. What was the point in having power if you had to treat the peasant class with common courtesy? Still, Lim wasn't an idiot; his people weren't suicidal.

And there was still the Turkish bath on Boulevard du Port-Royal to think of. One survivor had described a gunman in a ski mask, but the shooter hadn't spoken, and the witness had been clubbed before he had a chance to focus on his adversary's eyes to see what shape they were.

If there was war, it pleased Dupin to think that he would win. His soldiers would be fighting on their own home ground—the next best thing to Corsica, at any rate—and it was *his* connections to police and judges that the Triads found so necessary to continuing their operations. If it came down to a killing choice, Dupin was quite prepared to pull strings with the police and have Lim's people thrown in jail. He knew enough to run them ragged if he dropped some well-placed hints and sent the Sûreté on a hunt for Triad heroin connections. It would hurt Dupin, of course, deplete his revenue somewhat until the storm blew over, but he was prepared to sacrifice for victory.

And for revenge.

He had to think about the problem for a bit before he started taking any action. If Lim wasn't responsible for the attack on Heuse, then it would be a grave mistake to strike back at the 14K. Dupin would have to reach out for his spies around the city and see what he could learn about the incident. Once he reliably identified the man or men responsi-

ble, he would unleash such fury that the hitters would be sorry they were ever born.

He might wipe out their families, too, for fun—and to ensure that there was no protracted blood feud waiting for him somewhere down the road.

"I want the soldiers ready," Dupin said. "All of them, no excuses. If the Chinese think they can take over Paris just like that, we'll have a big surprise for Monsieur Lim."

"You think it might be someone else?"

"I'm not prepared to say. Someone believes that he can sweep us to the side like so much garbage. We must find out who's responsible before we educate him in the nature of his fatal error."

"If it's Lim," Heuse said, "I want the slant-eyed bastard for myself."

"If we're at war with the Chinese," Dupin replied, "there'll be enough to go around. You needn't be afraid of missing out."

"Just so you know."

His second-in-command was blustering to cover up the fear he had to have felt when bodyguards were dropping all around him, spilling brains and blood across the sidewalk. It was only natural for such a man as Heuse to feel his manhood challenged by a sneak attack where he was forced to run away. They would be better off, though—closer to their goal—when Heuse started thinking with his head, instead of with his balls.

"I've heard you, Leon. Now hear me. We can't afford mistakes this time. If anyone—and I mean *anyone*—moves against Lim before we're sure that he's to blame, I'll have the bastard's head. You understand me, Leon?"

"But of course."

"Good. See to your soldiers, then. I want them ready at a moment's notice. When the time comes, we'll need every man we have."

And then some, Dupin thought, but he was smiling confidently as his chief lieutenant left the room. It didn't pay to sweat in front of your subordinates.

The sneaky bastards might begin to get ideas.

And that would never do.

KATZ DREW THE TRIAD BEAT because he was the only multilingual member of the team, his fluency in French enhanced by study at the Sorbonne in his younger days, before he'd donned a uniform for the Israeli government. If any one of them could pass as French—or Corsican—and thus persuade the Triads that their grudging allies were prepared to run amok, it would be Katz.

His first stop was the Jiang-you Club, a block north of the Parc Monceau. He wore an Uzi submachine gun underneath his belted trench coat, thought of topping the disguise off with a black beret, but finally decided he was pushing it. If all went well, the Triad targets he allowed to live would have no doubt their hangout had been raided by the Corsican Milieu.

The place was under guard when Katz arrived, not open to the gambling public yet. So much the better, leaving the civilians out of it. He drove past the club, parked on a side street and walked back along an alley redolent of urine. Stray cats flitted out of sight behind the battered trash cans as he passed. The two sentries on the back door looked bored, and Katz was ready for them by the time they noticed him, his left hand wrapped around the silenced Browning autoloader in the outside pocket of his coat.

Katz drew and fired in one smooth motion from a range of twenty feet. His first round struck the taller of the gunmen in the throat, all fight evaporating as the young man had to concentrate on drawing breath. He stumbled backward, slumped against the wall and slithered down the grimy brick into a seated posture, quickly going limp as oxygen and life ran out.

By that time Katz had nailed his partner with a second round between the eyes and was reaching for the doorknob with the metal claw that had replaced his right hand decades earlier.

Two guns on the door meant it was safe to leave unlocked, or so the Triads had supposed. Katz stepped across the threshold and closed the door behind him, leaving just a crack to hasten his retreat, if need be. Voices led him down a corridor until he reached the gaming room, where nine or ten young Chinese soldiers were collected, several of them grouped at two small tables while the others lined the bar.

"Monsieur Dupin sends greetings from the Corsican Milieu," Katz said in French, his voice raised so all of them could hear him. Whether they would understand was something else.

He hosed death along the bar, watching human targets sprawl before the stream of parabellum manglers. Tracking on, he found the gunmen at the tables scrambling to their feet, all reaching for their weapons, trying desperately to shave the round-eye's edge.

He didn't need to kill them all—indeed, it would defeat his purpose if at least one gunner didn't survive to spread the story of a killer spouting French—but there was no time for precision work, with half a dozen pistols jerking into view. Katz swept the killing ground from right to left and back again, his bullets ripping flesh, bone and fabric, smashing glass and gouging plaster. One of his opponents got a shot off, then another, but the rounds went high and wide as the gunners were cut down in their tracks.

When it was done, the smell of cordite sharp in Katzenelenbogen's nostrils, he reloaded and began a cursory examination of his enemies. Three of the nine were breathing, but one of those was so badly wounded that he would inevitably bleed to death before an ambulance arrived. As for the other two...

Katz made the call himself, the French equivalent of 911, and told the operator what had happened more or less. She asked his name, and for the hell of it Katz said, "François Dupin."

It wouldn't stick, of course, and that was fine. He didn't want Dupin arrested, locked away beyond the line of fire. It was enough that questions should be raised, suspicion cultivated. In the short run, which was all that mattered, Toh Lim would be looking for a scapegoat, grasping at the most convenient and most logical of enemies.

TOH LIM SLAMMED DOWN the telephone with force enough to make his fingers ache. Bad news and more bad news was all he heard this day. At least this time there was a chance his soldiers hadn't died in vain. One babbled to police as they were hauling him away for surgery, and while delirium had left the message garbled, Lim was crystal clear about the name.

Dupin.

The Corsican had to be insane to pull a stunt like this. What was he thinking? *Was* he thinking? Could it be that he was using some of the narcotics he had smuggled for so long? Drugs killed the brain or left it twisted, next to useless.

How else to explain a man who would betray his business partners and provoke a shooting war for no good reason?

It wasn't as if Dupin could hope to seize the Triad family for himself. By waging war against the 14K, he barred himself from dealing China white in any worthwhile quantity, and guaranteed that Lim would take the necessary steps to have him killed. Of course, Dupin had troops, but they were spread across the country, many of them in Marseilles, where the narcotics labs were refining heroin from opium and cutting it for resale on the streets. In Paris he would have perhaps 150 soldiers—still a solid number, but it placed

his edge at roughly two-to-one, instead of several times that number.

Even through the anger, Lim was still confused and curious about the earlier attacks Dupin and Leon Heuse had suffered in the city. What did *that* mean? Was there some connection to the Corsican assault upon the Jiang-you Club? It made no sense.

Forget it!

Who could understand barbarians? Their minds weren't the same as those of civilized Chinese. Impulsive, stupid actions were their stock-in-trade, and when they suffered from a bout of rowdy negligence, they looked for scapegoats, someone who could take the blame while they took on a pose of injured innocence. Duplicity was second nature to the round-eyes, but they weren't much good at laying out conspiracies. Too busy thinking with their genitals and putting faith in muscle over mind.

For all that, Lim was still embarrassed that the Corsicans had managed to surprise him. He should have prepared himself, anticipated treachery, and cut them off before his losses started mounting up. Already he had lost sufficient men that it would jeopardize his chances of a victory. The odds weren't yet impossible, but he would have to go on the offensive, strike back swiftly and with force enough to crush the Corsicans before they could inflict more damage on his army.

Lim hesitated, thinking of the past week's violence in London, Amsterdam and North America. He couldn't blame the Corsicans for those attacks, but what if there was something larger, more insidious afoot? Suppose the Triads' several round-eyed allies—from the Mafia and the Camorra, maybe even the Colombians—were joining ranks in an attempt to seize the Asian pipeline for themselves?

It was a fool's game, but the world was full of idiots. Five minutes browsing through the newspaper would drive that lesson home. How many wars were raging at the moment

over childish grudges, simple greed or racial and religious bigotry? Who ever went to war believing he would lose?

It was a subject Lim could take up with his hill chief when they next had time to speak. Right now he had his hands full with an enemy who had superb connections to the justice system, who was fighting on his native soil and who had never lost a major war. If you looked back at history, the Corsicans could even boast of an alliance with the CIA.

What if...?

He wouldn't chase that line of thought or let himself get bogged down in a search for phantom enemies. The ones who stood before him were enough to occupy his mind, and then some. If he lost his grip, allowed himself to weaken, they would plow him under, finish him.

But Toh Lim wasn't finished yet. He wasn't immortal, granted, but he *was* a warrior, skilled at overcoming opposition from his enemies.

François Dupin had made the worst mistake of his misguided life.

With any luck at all, it would turn out to be the last.

MACK BOLAN PEERED through the telescopic sight attached to his Galil sniping rifle. Across Rue Cardinet he had a clear view through the spacious windows of a fifth-floor office. Half a dozen men in shiny suits were gesticulating as they argued, jabbing fingers at one another in their eagerness to make a point.

He couldn't read their lips, since they were speaking Cantonese, but Bolan knew roughly what they were saying. There could be only one main topic of discussion in the Triad ranks: the losses they had suffered since the sun came up that morning and the "evidence" suggesting Corsicans had staged those raids.

The two sides hadn't started killing one another yet, but it wouldn't be long if Bolan and his Phoenix Force warriors stirred the pot sufficiently, then brought it to a rolling boil.

In fact, he had a dash of seasoning for the hellacious recipe right now.

The folding-stock Galil fed 7.62 mm NATO rounds from a detachable 20-round box magazine. It was a semiautomatic weapon, inasmuch as snipers normally weren't inclined to hose down their targets when they could do a clean, precision job instead.

It didn't matter much if he killed every soldier in the office or hit none at all. The very fact of the assault would be another thorn in Lim's flesh, another goad to make him rise and fight the Corsicans. And while the predators were eating one another alive, there should be time for Bolan to step in, find Sheng and sever one more link between the 14K and mainland China.

First things first.

He chose a target, placed the cross hairs on his chosen victim's face and stroked the trigger. Death exploded from the muzzle of his weapon at 2,674 feet per second, bridging the hundred-foot gap between sniper and target in a fraction of a heartbeat. Bolan was lining up his second shot even as the office window shivered, sprouting spiderweb designs, and the first Triad went down in a spray of crimson, missing half his face.

He barely kept track after that. Two up, two down, and then he put two bullets through a globe that stood atop a filing cabinet to his left. Round five took down another Triad soldier, nearly ripping off his arm.

The Executioner kept firing, choosing marks without regard to whether they were animate or bits of furniture. He raked the full length of the room twice over, left four bodies stretched out on the floor and two more huddled under cover, praying for a lucky break.

They got it when his magazine ran empty, and he backed off from the ledge to stow his weapon out of sight, prepared to take his leave.

It wouldn't be much longer now, the way he was turning up the heat in Paris. Bolan only hoped he would be ready when the lid blew off. Too many chefs, he realized, could spoil the broth.

And one of them could wind up getting scalded in the bargain, if he didn't watch his ass.

Leon Heuse was happy to be on the street again. It had been years since he was cast in the position of a lowly soldier, riding into battle with the Milieu's enemies, but this was personal. The men he was looking for had shamed him in the public eye, killed four men while he stood and watched, then chased him from the street outside his own apartment building like some frightened child.

A debt like that had to be repaid in kind.

Heuse occupied the front seat of a Citroën sedan, beside the driver, with three men behind him in the back seat. Five more gunners occupied a second car, all of them armed with pistols and MAT 49 submachine guns, the 9 mm weapons designed for colonial service after the Second World War but still functional and deadly on an urban battlefield. Eight men, not counting drivers, could unload 260 rounds in six or seven seconds flat if necessary, all without resorting to their side arms.

It should be enough for the Chinese.

Dupin had finally climbed down off the fence an hour earlier, when two young gunmen, obviously 14K, had walked into a barbershop on Rue Lecourbe and opened fire with sawed-off shotguns at the patron in the center chair. Antoine Chagal, a childhood crony of Dupin, was nearly cut in two by buckshot, and the war was on in earnest.

"Turn left here at the light," Heuse told his driver.

Their target, first of several, was a Chinese pawnshop on Rue Poncelet. It fronted for a loan-shark operation, doling out money to Chinese businessmen or home owners in need, extracting interest on a scale of twenty-five percent per week. The penalties for tardy payment were extreme.

Heuse had no quarrel with loan sharks as a rule; he'd done some sharking of his own, in fact, and never minded breaking arms or heads when someone fell behind in paying off their rightful debt. He hated Asians, though—a fact related to his father's death in Indochina in the early 1950s. Heuse was still an infant at the time, but he had grown up hearing all about the fallen hero and the men who killed him. The Vietnamese were not Chinese, of course, but Leon Heuse wasn't an anthropologist.

To Heuse, gooks were gooks, and those who tried to blow his head off on the street outside his own apartment house were asking for the kind of trouble most men didn't survive.

"Up there," he told the driver, pointing. "On the left."

Heuse and his soldiers stepped from their cars, each brandishing a submachine gun, while the drivers kept their engines running, with a sharp eye on the rearview mirror, watching out for police. They crossed the pavement to the sidewalk, lining up no more than ten or twelve feet from the plate glass window of the shop.

Inside, the elderly proprietor saw trouble coming, ducked behind his counter and lay facedown on the floor. He didn't know these men, but understood what had been happening in Chinatown the past few hours, and the guns they carried ruled out any brief thought of heroics.

"Fire!"

Eight guns went off in unison, staccato thunder echoing from shop fronts on the other side, behind the firing squad. They trashed the pawnshop and a major portion of its inventory in the time it took to wind a watch, 9 mm bullets streaming through the door and window, drilling abstract

patterns in the walls, exploding glass showcases, toppling merchandise displays. Spent cartridges lay all around the gunners when they finished, pale sunlight glinting on the brass.

Heuse would have liked to go inside and see if there was anyone still living in the shop, but he had other stops to make, and someone would have called the police by now. If they stood still for any length of time, arrests were probable, and Heuse would miss most of the targets on his hit list.

That would never do.

He turned back toward the waiting cars, barking orders at his men. They followed him, some of them smiling, loving it.

Why not?

Man was a hunter by his very nature. Anything that "civilized" him dulled that edge, resulted in a corresponding lack of strength and energy.

It was good to be hunting again, Heuse thought. It felt right.

THE SMALL APARTMENT building on Rue de Prony wasn't much to look at: solid, well maintained but nothing fancy, nothing to suggest the tenants were a breed apart. In fact, Bolan thought, most of them were doubtless ordinary citizens who held down jobs, went on vacation in the summertime and kept their indiscretions out of public view.

One tenant didn't fit the mold, however, and it was the maverick Bolan came to see.

Marcel Bouchet had told him where to find Tu Sheng, and only pressing need had kept the Executioner from making it the first stop on his list. Now it was pushing noon, and Bolan felt like having Sheng for lunch. A little Chinese appetizer, leading to the main course later on.

He entered through the lobby, paused to check the mailbox for 5C, but there was no card in the slot provided to display a tenant's name. Sheng liked his privacy, and that

was fine. The traveling ambassador of the People's Revolution couldn't be too careful these days, in a world where die-hard Communists were posted to a spot on the endangered-species list.

He took the stairs, considering the risk of soldiers waiting for him up on the fifth floor. He was prepared for anything, in theory, and he wouldn't mind if some of Lim's people had to fall before he reached Sheng. It was a long time coming, this appointment with the fixer from Beijing, and anyone who tried to stop him now was asking for a one-way trip to hell.

The access door on the fifth floor was blind, no window, and he barged through as if he owned the place, his Uzi cocked and ready. There was no one in the hall, no noise to speak of emanating from behind the eight numbered doors, four on each side of the hall.

He held the submachine gun ready as he walked to 5C and spent a moment listening. No sound at all seeped from the apartment, and he felt his stomach knotting with a sudden pang of déjà vu. The silence didn't mean that Sheng was gone. He could be resting, reading, staring out the window—anything at all. If he was on his own, so much the better.

A swift kick snapped the lock, and Bolan charged across the threshold, covering the vacant living room and kitchen, sweeping on from there to check the bedrooms, double back and hit the bathroom just in case.

Goddammit!

There were no convenient notes this time, but Sheng hadn't packed up his belongings, either. There were clothes in the closet, with an empty suitcase; socks and underwear in dresser drawers; a toothbrush and assorted other items in the bathroom. If Sheng was running this time, he had set some kind of record for traveling light.

Bolan thought of waiting, just to see if Sheng came back, but ruled it out at once. He had already caused too much

commotion, booting in the door, and Sheng could be away from home for hours.

Bolan couldn't spare the time to sit around and wait for him. At best he would be wasting precious hours, dumping too much work on his comrades from Phoenix Force. At worst he would be sitting there when the police arrived to haul him in, and that would be the end of everything.

His second thought, as he was moving toward the open door, involved a thermite canister, but Sheng could always get new clothes and toiletries, while the potential damage to his neighbors would be catastrophic.

Scratch Plan B.

That brought him back to Toh Lim, the godfather of Chinatown. If he couldn't find Sheng, at least there was no shortage of alternate targets in Paris. His plan was working like a charm so far, with the Corsicans and Triads snapping at each other's throats. But Bolan didn't want to let his enemies do all the work while he stood idly by and watched them from the sidelines.

Exiting the flat, he heard a muffled gasp behind him and turned to find a gray-haired woman gaping at him from the doorway of her own apartment.

"No one home," he told her, noting that her gaze was focused on the SMG. He didn't know if she could understand a word he said, but there was no harm trying.

"If you see my old friend Mr. Sheng," he said, "feel free to tell him I'll be back."

MARCEL BOUCHET WAS SEATED in his tiny sixth-floor office on the Quai d'Orsay, a scanner whispering the calls that had continued almost without letup since the crack of dawn. Bouchet had lost track of the dead, had no more energy for keeping track of shooting calls, explosions, new reports of speeding cars and bodies scattered on the street.

He should be out there doing something, but he couldn't think of anything to do. The violence was as much his fault

as anyone's, considering the information he had passed to the American, but it was hard for him to work up any sense of guilt. There were no innocents among the dead so far, which helped, but but he was not so sure it would have changed his mind in any case.

His bitterness had been a long time building, watching as the men he was supposed to put away ran roughshod over everyone and everything in sight. The Corsicans at first, and then the Chinese. Colombians had started turning up the past two years or so, and while the Sûreté removed some dealers from the street, there was no shortage of replacements waiting in the wings, no lasting injury inflicted on the syndicate.

Until today.

It shouldn't be like this, he told himself. It shouldn't have to be.

But there it was.

Unfortunately syndicated crime had reached the point where leaders of the network were effectively untouchable by lawful means. There was no widespread history of vigilantism in France—not since the Reign of Terror, at least—but maybe it was time to throw the rules away.

No, that was wrong, but they could take a brief vacation from procedure—just a day or two—to clean the streets of human garbage. Start fresh in the morning, with a brand-new, level playing field.

What would the Yankees say? Fat chance.

It seemed that the advantage always lay with Bouchet's enemies. They had more money, to begin with, and there were no rules or regulations for the other side. They could do anything that came to mind: bribe cops and judges, murder witnesses, you name it.

There would never be a level playing field as long as those who fought for law and order were compelled to dot their *i*'s and cross their *t*'s, while their opponents couldn't even spell. And it felt good to watch them scramble for their lives, these

animals who preyed on other members of the human race like ruthless cannibals. Today was their turn on the menu, and Bouchet could only hope fear ate them up alive.

Those who survived.

He hardly thought about himself, having already worked through the initial moments of concern as to his fate if anyone found out that he had helped Belasko set this chain of grim events in motion. There were worse things than disgrace, the loss of a position where he managed to accomplish nothing on the average day.

The office suddenly felt stifling, almost claustrophobic. Rather than a place to hide from trouble and responsibility, as it had been in recent months, his cubicle felt like a cage. Bouchet wished he could be out on the street, with Belasko and the others—whoever *they* were—carrying the battle to their common enemy, and never mind the cost.

Bouchet thought that he should have been a soldier, and smiled at that. He *had* been once, but that was long ago, before the rules and regulations beat him down and broke his will to strive. Too many years of watching as the bad guys won and laughed at justice had reduced him to the status of a simple bookkeeper, what the Americans would call a bean counter. Except Bouchet was busy counting other things: narcotics shipments, brothels, teenage addicts, lifeless bodies in the gutter.

It was time to turn the game around and let the heavies take a beating for a change. But did he have the nerve to play that game?

Damned right!

He checked his pistol, made sure it was ready and returned it to the holster on his belt. The scanner in his car would tell him where to go once he was rolling. There was action all around him on this afternoon of blood and thunder. All he had to do was make himself available, be in the right place at the proper time.

IT WAS HIS LAST, best chance to slip away, Sheng realized while Toh Lim was playing soldier with his troops. Sheng couldn't fathom why a man like Lim would rush away to lead the next raid by himself, but the most recent Corsican attacks had stung his "host" like bitter nettles. Lim had gone off muttering about his honor, speaking in a voice so soft that Sheng gave up on understanding him before Lim reached the door.

Whatever happened on the streets in the next few hours, Sheng recognized a chance to save himself, and he wasn't about to let it slip away. He had his passport in his pocket, credit cards and cash, nothing to pack before he fled Lim's house.

Assuming that the guards would let him leave.

Sheng had no way of knowing what their orders were, whether they had been instructed to protect him or make sure that he didn't escape. The only way to find out, he decided, was to try.

He left Lim's study, wandered through the kitchen, dining room and living room before he found the houseman, just returning from a tour of the grounds.

"I'm ready," Sheng informed him. "Where's the car?"

The houseman blinked at him, confused. "What car?" he asked.

Sheng rolled his eyes, a man exasperated by incompetence. "I'm going to the airport," he replied. "Were you not told?"

"The airport?"

"I've been ordered back to Hong Kong," he informed the man. There was no point telling anyone where he was really going, for a while. "I leave now, at once, or I will miss my flight."

"No one said anything to me," the houseman said. "I'll have to ask."

"By all means ask." Sheng's voice dripped venom. "I'm sure your master won't mind being interrupted in the mid-

dle of a war to have his orders questioned. He will certainly congratulate you for your diligence."

The houseman obviously didn't think so, mulling that one over for a moment, frowning at the effort generated by decision making.

"I don't need to call him," the man said after due reflection. "He has more-important things to think about. I'll fetch the driver."

Sheng would much rather have acted as his own chauffeur, but that would raise suspicion in the houseman's mind, perhaps convince him that he should call Lim, after all. It would be simple to dismiss the driver once they reached the airport. In the midst of so much action and intrigue, no soldier of the 14K would care to waste his time in the departure lounge at Orly when he could be angling for a chance to hit the street.

Five minutes later Sheng was on his way...but not to Hong Kong. Not just yet.

Sheng didn't think the Dragon would be pleased to see him on a day like this, with so much trouble in the air. He needed someplace to cool off, relax awhile and clear his head.

He knew the perfect place, and it wasn't so very far away.

FRANÇOIS DUPIN WAS READY when his enemies arrived. It startled him a bit that they would dare attack his home on Rue Henri Barbusse, in Clichy, but the leader of the Corsican Milieu hadn't survived this long by being unprepared. His guards were posted when the Chinese started to arrive—six carloads of them, he was told—and there were ample guns on hand to give them all the action they were looking for.

That was what he got, the French-born mobster told himself, for dealing with a gang of slant-eyed savages as if they were normal men.

His bigotry was automatic, a conditioned reflex, but it didn't cloud his thinking on strategic matters. Whether they were Asian, black or native born, Dupin would never underestimate his enemies. The quickest way to die, aside from trusting so-called friends, was to persuade yourself that enemies were weak and stupid, easily defeated on the basis of their class, race, dialect, religion—anything, in fact, except their proved willingness to kill. The aristocracy had made that grave mistake in France two hundred years earlier, and thousands of them wound up on the guillotine as a result. "Let them eat cake," the lady had said, and then her head was lying in a wicker basket, like a melon fresh from harvest.

The Chinese were proved killers, and Dupin respected that. He hated them no less for their abilities, of course, but he wouldn't permit his soldiers to get cocky and deceive themselves with fantasies of easy victory.

In fact, Dupin decided, as the first shots echoed from the general direction of his wrought-iron gates, it would be best if he went out to lead the troops himself, set an example for the men who were prepared to kill—or die—on his behalf.

"Armand!" he snapped, and waited for his houseman to report.

"Yes, sir?"

"Find me a weapon quickly! And tell the men I'm coming out to join them."

"Sir?"

"Right now!"

"Yes, sir!"

Dupin felt better as he recognized the old familiar thrill of battle radiating from his groin to light a fire inside him. He felt ten years younger, standing there. His enemies were waiting for him, issuing their challenge, like the good old days.

The leader of the Corsican Milieu didn't intend to keep them waiting long.

THE RADIO ALERT CAME as Bouchet was driving south on Avenue George V. He made a screeching U-turn in the middle of the street, almost colliding with a taxi in the process. But he had the blue light flashing on his dashboard by the time he started north, reversing his direction toward suburban Clichy.

It could only be Dupin's estate; there were no other likely targets on the high-priced residential street of Rue Henri Barbusse. And if Dupin's estate was under fire, then it could only mean his enemies were out in force.

That, in its turn, could only mean the Triads had gone looking for revenge. Belasko's crazy plot was working, maybe better than the tall American had dared to hope. Would he—or the police—be able to control the conflagration that was raging through the streets of Paris? Would the city be forever scarred by what took place this day?

Or would it be swept clean?

The drive to Clichy took nearly fifteen minutes, even with the light and siren clearing traffic from his path. French drivers were a stubborn lot, as well as reckless, some of them preferring to show insolence in any face-off with authority. A couple of patrol cars reached the scene before Bouchet arrived. The officers in uniform were pinned down by automatic-weapons fire, one of them stretched out on the street as Bouchet skidded to a halt and bailed out of his vehicle, the Walther P-5 automatic ready in his hand.

The wrought-iron gates were open. A luxury sedan was stalled between them, bullet scarred and empty, three doors standing open with their windows shattered, and a dead man was lying on the ground beside the car. Some other vehicles had obviously made their way inside, and a Mercedes-Benz had been cut off when the preceding vehicle was ambushed and disabled. It, too, was abandoned, doors wide open where the soldiers had evacuated, rushing in to face Dupin's reserves on foot.

Bouchet ducked as another swarm of bullets rattled overhead. He didn't need to check the fallen officer for vital signs; the young man's face was gone, and blood had pooled beneath his body, spreading like a crimson inkblot on the pavement. The surviving officers looked to Bouchet with mingled fear and hope, prepared to let him take control and save them if he could.

"How many guns inside?" he asked of no one in particular.

"At least four cars besides these two," the nearest uniform responded. "There were five or six men in each car. Chinese, I think."

"You know whose house this is?"

The three survivors nodded jerkily. They knew François Dupin by reputation, never dreaming that his path would cross their own, much less in such a way as this.

"We have to get inside," Bouchet informed them. "Have you called for help?"

"First thing. You're all that's come so far."

"We can't wait any longer," Bouchet said. "There are people getting killed in there. We have to try and stop it."

Or, he thought, at least help with the killing.

"Will you follow me?"

They hesitated, finally gave the jerky nods a second time. Bouchet crept forward, peered around the fender of the car that sheltered him and glimpsed a Triad soldier with a submachine gun stepping out to get a better shot at the police. Bouchet was ready for him, squeezing off two rounds that struck his target in the upper chest and slammed him over backward, sprawling on the close-cut grass.

"Let's go!"

He didn't wait to see if anyone would follow him, but started sprinting toward the open gates, his pistol held in front of him. A second Chinese gunner popped out on his right, prepared to fire, then went down squirming on the deck as Bouchet shot him in the face.

So far so good.

Six rounds remained in his pistol, plus the two spare magazines he carried, which made twenty-four in all. On impulse, he swerved to his left and grabbed the fallen hardman's submachine gun, noting that it was the short Beretta Model 12S with a folding metal stock. An extra magazine protruded from the dead man's belt, and Bouchet claimed it for himself.

"Come on," he told the uniforms, already moving up the driveway. "We don't want to miss the show."

IT WAS A GAMBLE, going in when the police were surely on their way, if not already on the scene, but Bolan was prepared to take the risk. He left his car behind Dupin's estate, on a smaller residential street, and went in from the rear, scaling the retaining wall and homing in on the sounds of combat.

One benefit of arriving late was obvious at once: Dupin's sentries had been drawn from their posts to meet the raiders at the gate. It left the rear wide open, and he met no opposition on his long run toward the house.

All hell had broken loose out front, with automatic weapons hammering, their long bursts punctuated by the sound of shotgun blasts and pistol fire. As Bolan worked his way around the east side of the house, he heard male voices, scared or angry, shouting in Chinese and French. He didn't have to guess what they were saying, having been in combat countless times himself, where men he knew as friends were cursing, shouting questions, giving orders, challenging their enemies or asking help from a long-forgotten God. Few who survived this day would harbor any clear-cut memories of what they said or did while they were fighting for their lives, and it would make no difference to the ones who died.

He cleared the final corner, scanned the field and saw perhaps a dozen Corsicans spread out in front of Dupin's house, some crouched behind a pair of limousines parked

in the drive, while others found their shelter behind marble pillars on the porch. Fifteen or twenty Chinese gunmen were returning fire, split up in squads of four or five men each that hid behind their own disabled vehicles a few yards farther out. The raiding force had closed to point-blank range before they stalled, and they were matching the defenders burst for burst, unable and unwilling to retreat.

Was that Toh Lim behind the nearest Triad vehicle? It seemed unlikely that the red pole would turn out to lead a raid himself, but stranger things had happened in the Executioner's experience. That crouching figure on the far side of the porch was certainly François Dupin, come out to join his soldiers in a last-ditch stand against his enemies. As Bolan watched, the leader of the Corsican Milieu squeezed off a burst of submachine gun fire and knocked a Chinese gunner sprawling on the blacktop drive.

Bolan removed a frag grenade from his belt and yanked the pin, then sidearmed the bomb toward the broad front porch. One of the Corsicans glimpsed movement from the corner of his eye, squeezed off a burst at Bolan without aiming, but the rounds were off by six or seven feet. Before the shooter could correct his aim, the grenade went off and swept the porch with shrapnel, leaving bodies sprawled on blood-streaked marble as the shock wave passed.

One of the Chinese gave a shout, and several of them rose from cover firing, as if Bolan's blast had been a signal to attack. The Corsicans behind the two black limousines were torn between surprise at the explosion and determination to annihilate their enemies. Most of them started firing at the Triad gunners, but a pair of Corsican hardmen ran back toward the porch, as if to find out what had happened and see if they could help.

The Executioner was waiting for them, stepping over dead and wounded, firing with his Uzi from the hip. He tagged one on the steps and cut the other's legs from under him just

as he reached the landing, dropping him facedown on the porch.

A second frag grenade sailed high across the few surviving Corsicans, bounced once atop the car where Toh Lim or his look-alike was hiding and rolled out of sight before it blew. This time a cheer went up in French, and Bolan watched the handful of defenders break from cover, charging toward their adversaries, closing in a rush as they poured automatic fire into the Chinese ranks.

It was a massacre as the last few soldiers grappled hand to hand. Three or four Chinese broke ranks and raced back toward the gates, but they were cut down on the run. The man who shot them likewise fell, a bullet smashing through his skull. The firing sputtered out and was replaced by sirens wailing in the distance, closing in from all points of the compass.

Bolan saw François Dupin, a broken mannequin, his face and torso ripped by shrapnel from the first grenade. He turned away, glanced back across the battlefield and froze at sight of a familiar face.

Marcel Bouchet was slumped against the second Triad car in line, one hand clasped to his bloody side, a submachine gun dangling from the other. A younger uniformed man beside him saw Bolan watching from the porch and raised a pistol, but Bouchet reached out to strike the weapon down. He spoke in French, and Bolan watched the uniform retreat, move back along the line of cars until he reached another pair of men in blue, sprawled facedown on the pavement.

"So, you made it," Bouchet said as he approached.

"You, too."

"I think so. There's more blood than pain so far. A flesh wound, I suspect."

"Good luck."

"The same to you," Bouchet replied. "You'll need it if you linger here much longer."

"I'm already gone."

"One thing. There is a man you seek?"

"You know there is."

"I checked before I left the office," Bouchet said. "He was with Lim before all this, but now he's running. Flying, I should say. You'll find him in Marseilles if you are quick enough."

"I owe you one."

"Next time you're in Paris, you can buy the wine." Bouchet was smiling as he spoke. "We'll find some women, drink too much and lie about heroic deeds."

"Sounds good to me. I'll see you."

"*Au revoir,*" the Frenchman said before he closed his eyes.

9

Marseilles

Marseilles had always been a major port of entry for heroin and other contraband making its way into France. The nation's second-largest city, with a population of eight hundred thousand full-time residents, Marseilles was also France's largest port on the Mediterranean Sea, an easy run from Corsica, Sardinia or Sicily. The uncut opium that came in through Marseilles had traditionally been Turkish, supplemented by a steady flow of hashish from Morocco and Algiers, but changing times brought a taste of China white to southern France, along with South American cocaine. The Triads were entrenched around Marseilles these days, and their alliance with the Corsican Milieu allowed them to survive without a major shooting war.

At least, it had before the Executioner and company arrived.

The warehouse was a 1950s-vintage structure, dating from the era of the Marshall Plan, when the United States was pouring money into Western Europe in a bid to dam the tide of postwar communism and revolt against established governments that had been weakened by the Nazi occupation. Touch-ups with a paintbrush didn't hide the fact that it was aging badly, like a tired old sailor who still craved the rolling sea but couldn't quite keep his wits about him on dry land.

Some thermite, Bolan calculated, and the whole damned place would burn as if it were made of cardboard soaked in gasoline. The drugs inside, delivered yesterday and waiting on a transfer to the local cutting plant, would be a total loss.

A short flight of steps painted green brought Bolan to the loading dock. He tried the first door that he came to, felt it open at his touch and stepped inside. He was greeted by cool darkness, with a bare bulb several yards in front of him, its dim light barely adequate to cut the murk. He followed voices speaking in Cantonese, and was about to turn the corner on the warehouse proper when a young Chinese approaching from the opposite direction blundered into him, rebounding with a startled gasp.

The Uzi stuttered, delivering three quick rounds, and Bolan had no time to watch his target fold. He went around the corner in a rush, found three more Chinese gaping at him, frozen for a heartbeat by the shocking sounds of gunfire.

It was all he needed.

Bolan wasn't taking any prisoners today. He stitched the trio with a burst of parabellum manglers and dropped them where they stood. He remained in place another moment, waiting, just in case there might be someone he had missed among the stacked-up crates of merchandise downrange. When no one surfaced after fifteen seconds, Bolan tucked away his SMG and took the first of several thermite canisters out of his raincoat's sagging pockets.

There was no great trick to burning down a structure, regardless of its composition or construction standards, if you had the right materials on hand. White phosphorus, exposed to air, burned with a searing heat that water wouldn't quench; it ate through concrete, granite, tempered steel and human flesh with fine impartiality, requiring special chemicals to douse the blaze. It was the perfect choice for military applications, and it did a fair job on civilian targets, too.

The thermite fire would leave no evidence to speak of, nothing that would point to any single arsonist, and that was fine. The shock waves spreading out from Paris would convince both sides—the Corsicans and Triads—that the war clouds had blown southward to Marseilles.

It didn't put him on the track of Tu Sheng—not yet, at least—but he was in the right vicinity. Sheng would be running, maybe stopping only long enough to grab some cash and hit the road again, but it was worth a shot. With an assist from Phoenix Force, he still might have a chance to pin down the ChiCom operator.

And if he missed Sheng in Marseilles, there was a whole wide world in which to track him down. Eventually the agent would be forced to run for home, and that was Bolan's final destination anyway.

The Executioner was riding this train to the end of the line.

THE CORSICAN GLANCED UP as Katz entered the lobby of the new apartment building, visibly relaxing as he saw the new arrival was Caucasian rather than Chinese. He didn't smile—it would have gone against the soldier's character—but he allowed himself a nod and went back to the nudie magazine he had been scrutinizing, tucked inside a newspaper to make it more politically correct in public.

"Shame on you," Katz said in French, the shooter glancing up with some confusion on his face as Katz produced his Browning autoloader with the silencer attached and punched a bullet through the lookout's forehead.

Simple.

There was no time to remove the body, but it hardly mattered. Even if a witness wandered in within the next few seconds, found the body and ran out to call police, Katz should be finished by the time the uniforms began converging on his target site.

If not, well, he would deal with that problem in its turn.

He rode the elevator up, glancing at his watch to confirm that he was on time. Precision counted with his chosen target; Louis Beltran was known for leaving home to head for the office every weekday on the stroke of half past eight. It was a failing no top-ranking mobster should cultivate if he wanted to survive, but years of peace and quiet in the neighborhood had deadened Beltran's built-in sense of paranoia that had kept him on the streets this long.

The capo of Marseilles was past due for a change.

Katz rode the elevator to the seventh floor, had the MP-5 K submachine gun cocked and ready as he left the elevator, reaching back to punch a button that would freeze the car in place until he finished with his business and was ready to evacuate the floor. He saw no lookouts, and moved toward number 721 with brisk, determined strides. The neighbors might be used to Beltran's hard-faced visitors by now, but they wouldn't be ready for this morning's call.

He found the door he wanted and took up station slightly to the left, out of view from anyone who checked the peephole before venturing out. He held the MP-5 K braced against his hip and prayed that Beltran would be punctual this morning, no delays to let a neighbor spot the ambush and run screaming for police before Katz had a chance to do his job.

It was 8:31 by Katzenelenbogen's watch when the door opened and a pair of burly gunners stepped into the hallway, one behind the other. Louis Beltran, smaller than his bodyguards and better dressed, was right behind them, while a fourth man came along behind to lock the door and double-check it with a jiggle of the knob. One of the leading soldiers had Katz spotted by that time. French curses poured from his lips, and he reached for his pistol, hidden in a shoulder rig somewhere underneath his trench coat and suit jacket.

Too late.

Katz held down the MP-5 K's trigger, unloading parabellum shockers at a cyclic rate of eight hundred rounds per minute. With a 30-round box magazine, that meant that he could fire nonstop for 2.3 seconds before his clip ran dry. A heartbeat, in the scheme of things, but it was all Katz needed this time out.

The storm of hollowpoints ripped through his four targets, slamming them against the door and wall, explosive impact pinning them upright until his ammunition was exhausted.

Katz fed the little SMG a brand-new magazine as he headed back toward the elevator, hot brass crunching underneath his soles. A sudden thought stopped him before he reached the waiting car, and he retreated, stood above the bodies long enough to palm a death card from the *I Ching* tarot deck and drop it faceup on the crimson ruin of Louis Beltran's chest.

A little something from the Triads once removed, to keep the pot boiling in Marseilles. It wouldn't qualify as subtle, but the Corsicans weren't deep thinkers for the most part, and events in Paris would dispose them to expect the worst of their purported Chinese allies.

Perfect.

Katz walked back to the elevator, whistling to himself. It had the makings of a grim yet productive day.

McCARTER KNEW A PROBLEM when he saw one. The underground parking garage offered plenty of cover, but its murky light and crowded parking aisles reduced his field of fire and made precision work essential. If he blew it this time, thought the former SAS commando, the defense would smother him.

So he would simply have to get it right.

His target—or the vehicle his target drove, to be exact—was a charcoal gray Mercedes-Benz four-door sedan, with deeply tinted windows. There was no one in the car yet, or

the engine would have been running, but he had a lookout spotted from the time he entered the garage—Chinese, midtwenties from the look of him. No hardware showed, but McCarter knew he would be armed, with everything that had gone down in Paris recently. In fact, his very presence in the cavernous garage meant his employer had to be taking extraordinary care to keep himself alive.

Not that it would do him any good.

McCarter was positioned above the Mercedes and twenty feet away, taking advantage of the split-level garage's construction. Crouching between two midsize sedans, he had a clear view of the Benz through a long triangular gap between his own floor and the ramp in front of him, which carried traffic to another level overhead. The field of fire was clear, the elevators just beyond his line of vision on the left. The Uzi submachine gun balanced on his knee was fitted with a silencer and loaded with a 32-round magazine.

He waited, starting to perspire, his armpits itching. Any time, McCarter thought. Let's get it done, boys.

The Briton hadn't bothered to memorize the target's name. The men who came out of the elevator and approached the Benz were marked to die, as long as they were Triad members. If he missed the big man somehow, it would all come out the same. Another flash of paranoia, turning up the heat on their opponents, bringing Marseilles to a rolling boil.

He heard the elevator now, a whining to his left, the soft clash as it settled into place. He didn't hear the door hiss open, but McCarter caught the sharp sound of approaching footsteps loud and clear. He knelt between the cars that gave him shelter, raised the Uzi, aiming over open sights.

The lookout straightened to a rough approximation of attention, waiting for the others to approach. Two gunners had the lead, immediately followed by an older, shorter man, with one more soldier bringing up the rear to make it five in all. The Triad lookout who had been on station from

the first produced a set of keys and turned to pull the back door open for his boss.

McCarter saw his chance and seized it, squeezing off a burst that ripped the would-be driver's spine in two and dumped him forward on his face. He went down like a sack of groceries, spilling when he hit the pavement, going limp, with no attempt to rise or crawl away.

Scratch one.

The others were reacting like a team of trained professionals. One gave the boss a shove that took him out of sight behind the Benz, while his companions spun to face the calculated source of gunfire, reaching for the weapons stashed beneath their coats. McCarter gave them credit for a well-rehearsed attempt, but it wasn't enough to save their lives.

A whisper from the Uzi may have reached their ears, but the acoustics in the underground garage distorted even normal sounds, and they were working blind. Before they had a chance to spot him, the Briton unleashed another burst, his weapon tracking right to left, stitching them both with parabellum manglers. The taller of the two went over backward, triggering a pistol shot before he hit the deck, while his companion tottered toward the Benz, collapsed against its grille. He slid to his knees, one hand still clutching hardware, while the other tried to stanch the flow of blood from ragged stomach wounds.

Too late.

Another short burst caught him in the face and snapped his head back, blood and brains fanning out across the hood of the Mercedes like some kind of abstract paint job. He was inching to the floor as the surviving bodyguard reared up and fired two shots across the fender, scoring hits on glass and steel off to McCarter's right.

Another burst of parabellum shockers drove him under cover, but McCarter's time was running out. The Triad weapons had no silencers, and their reports rang out in the

garage like cannon fire. Someone was bound to hear the firing, and they would surely telephone for the police. Unless McCarter finished soon, he would be cornered, cut off from the street.

He reached inside the right-hand pocket of his raincoat, palmed a frag grenade and yanked the safety pin. It was a rather awkward pitch, despite the relatively easy range, but he could only try. The various alternatives—sit still and use up his ammo or try to flank the Benz on foot—were clearly unacceptable.

He lobbed the frag grenade, cursing roundly as it fell short and wobbled underneath the front end of the Benz. He had been trying for a clean bounce off the hood to put it in their laps.

When it blew, the charcoal gray Mercedes seemed to rear back like a prancing stallion, rising on a cloud of smoke and flame. Somebody screamed behind the vehicle, barely audible as it crashed back to earth, and though McCarter waited several seconds longer, hoping for a target he could sight on, there was nothing.

And he was out of time.

If people were still alive down there, they had to be wounded at the very least. Survivors might turn out to be a bonus, if they carried tales to keep the Corsican and Triad families at each other's throats.

He backed away, found the stairs and climbed four flights to reach the streets before he heard the first faint sound of sirens closing in the distance. It was part of the police experience that they habitually arrived too late to be of any help in crisis situations, short of picking up the bodies and reporting back to headquarters.

McCarter wished them well. Before the day was out, Marseilles police would have their hands full keeping track of corpses. And with any luck at all, McCarter's wouldn't be among them.

On the other hand . . .

He shrugged the morbid thought away and walked back to his car with long, swift strides. He had a job to do, and he was running out of time.

THE MARSEILLES safe-deposit box was one of several kept by Tu Sheng in European cities as diverse as London, Paris, Rome, Madrid and Amsterdam. There were thirteen in all, a number many Westerners would shun as an ill omen, but the agent from Beijing wasn't a slave to superstition. He believed, instead, that most bad luck was actually the product of poor planning, negligence or treachery. Preparedness meant standing ready to evacuate a given territory on a moment's notice, fleeing empty-handed if the situation called for desperate measures, taking whatever might be convenient if he had the time to pack.

Each safe-deposit box contained a passport, credit cards to match the given passport name, a loaded pocket pistol with an extra magazine and an ample amount of the local currency in large denominations. Sheng used different names at each and every bank, no correlation to the passport names, and had them memorized for use in an emergency.

Like now.

The teller was a young brunette who smelled like stale tobacco smoke. It was a fragrance Sheng expected of the French, competing with perfume, cologne and after-shave in this, a nation dedicated to its cigarettes. Her smile was charming, all the same, and Sheng replied in kind. She found the card he hadn't used since opening the box some thirteen months earlier, and watched him sign a false name on the proper line, beside her *X*. Sheng used his normal handwriting. He didn't plan to be in Marseilles long enough for anyone to check the many banks with a graphologist in tow.

She checked the signature, smiled once again and led him to the vault, where Sheng produced a key to match her own.

The box was fifteen inches deep, six inches square and weighed perhaps six pounds. The teller led him to a booth, much like a rest room stall, except that it contained a chair and table rather than a toilet. He waited while she closed the door behind her, checked the booth for spying cameras and finally opened up the box.

The passport was valid for another six years, and he would need it for only another week or so. The credit cards hadn't been used, although the fees were paid on time. The pistol was a four-inch Makarov, .380 caliber, inside a plastic sandwich bag. The crisp new francs were bundled with rubber bands, four thousand to a stack.

Sheng filled his pockets with the passport, credit cards, spare pistol magazine and cash. The Makarov was tucked inside his waistband at the back, where it was hidden by the full cut of his jacket. The plastic bag went back inside his safe-deposit box, a bit of mystery for anyone who followed him this far.

To hell with fingerprints.

Sheng's contact with the local Triad representatives had been minimal so far. He wasn't sure how much they knew about the mess in Paris, or the violence that had followed him from London, on through Amsterdam. There was a chance they would detain him if they blamed him for the death of Toh Lim, and Sheng wasn't prepared to let that happen—not when the elusive enemy was drawing closer all the time.

Already there were echoes of the battle in Marseilles. Sheng knew that he should call the Dragon, seek advice, but he was more concerned with personal survival at the moment. There would be enough time to consult with his superiors when he was safely out of France and on his way to...where?

The whole idea of safety had become a joke for Sheng in the past three days. He was becoming paranoid, and that wasn't the worst of it. Sheng knew his life was still in jeop-

ardy, would be until he managed to identify his enemies and help the Triads—or the Dragon—strike a killing blow against the round-eyes who had hunted him across three countries in as many days.

There was no time for that now, however. Sheng was still in danger. He could almost smell the battle smoke from where he stood, and instinct told him it wouldn't be long before his faceless adversaries found him in Marseilles. They were already in the city, if his judgment was correct. The shooting war between the Triads and Corsicans had been concocted as a ruse to spoil the Dragon's plans.

But why? By whom?

The answers still eluded Sheng, and he could only sort them out if he was still alive to think the problem through. Which meant that it was time for him to flee. Again.

A destination struck him as he stood there, waiting for the teller to return and lock away his safe-deposit box. There *was* a place where he might be secure. If he was wrong this time, at least his enemies would have their hands full with the locals while they tried to find Tu Sheng.

It would be worth a try.

The muscles of his face were cramped from so much scowling. It felt strange to smile again, but Sheng hung on to the expression as he left the bank and walked back to his waiting taxicab.

"The airport, driver."

Settling back to watch the traffic flow around him, Sheng decided it felt good to smile. He would remember that when all his enemies were dead and he was pissing on their graves.

THE TRIAD'S chief enforcer in Marseilles maintained an office on the sixth floor of a downtown building, with a long view of the waterfront through windows facing south. When guests stopped by to visit, Chin Sun was apt to offer wine and gourmet appetizers, fine cigars—perhaps a woman, if the visitor was male and had some extra time to kill in town.

Indeed, his hospitality was legendary in the province where he made his home these days, and he had been described on more than one occasion as an honorary Frenchman by his local friends.

This afternoon, though, Sun wasn't expecting guests. Instead, he was preparing to defend Marseilles and his investments on the 14K's behalf against the Corsicans who were supposed to be his allies. War had broken out between the criminal fraternities, and even though he didn't understand the reasons why, Sun wasn't prepared to play the loser's role.

Three of his chief lieutenants were assembled in the sixth-floor office to receive their orders, and he was waiting for the last one to arrive before he started laying out his plans. In two more minutes, if the tardy soldier hadn't shown his face, Sun would begin without him—and begin considering replacements for a man who kept his master waiting with no good excuse.

As if in answer to his thoughts, the office door swung open. Sun glanced up in time to see one of his bodyguards fly through the door headfirst and fall prone on the carpet. Close behind him, filling up the doorway, was a tall white man with a submachine gun in his hand.

Sun recoiled from the expression on the stranger's face and barked orders at his three lieutenants even as he dropped behind the desk to hide. His men were shouting, pushing back their chairs and scrambling for their weapons, taken absolutely by surprise. Sun heard the automatic weapon stutter, bullets striking flesh, walls, furniture. A high-pitched scream, somehow familiar, rang in Sun's ears, and something shattered on his desk—perhaps the photo of his wife and son he kept there, in a gilt-edged frame.

Sun wormed his way beneath the desk and into the knee hole, cringing as a body slammed against the desk, then slid away. The firing stopped in seconds flat, with no answer from his soldiers, and his only hope was that the gunman

would believe he had been killed outright in the initial firing. Or perhaps he would be overlooked in the excitement. How long could a stranger tarry in the circumstances, when he had to know help was on the way?

From where?

To come this far, the round-eye had to have dealt with those outside, perhaps the guards downstairs, as well. Was he a Corsican? He hadn't spoken yet, but Sun assumed—

A pair of black-clad legs came into view, their owner crouching, prodding Sun with the Uzi. "Get out of there," he ordered.

When Sun made no move to comply, strong fingers gripped his ankle, dragging him into the light as if he were a child. The gunman towered over him, a giant, peering down the barrel of his SMG.

"Speak English?"

Sun considered lying to him, but preferred to live a little longer if he could.

"I do."

"You know a man named Tu Sheng?"

Sun blinked. "What do you want with *him?*"

"I'll ask the questions, guy. Where is he?"

"In Marseilles."

The Uzi's muzzle pressed against his forehead, still uncomfortably warm.

"Let's try that one more time."

"He did not come to see me." Sun was trembling as he spoke. "I don't know why he came here, and he did not say how long he planned to stay."

"Where does he stay when he's in town?"

"Hotels," Sun answered. "Sheng has no apartment here."

"And you don't know where I can find him?"

"No."

"You're positive?"

"I swear."

"I guess we're finished, then."

Sun was starting to relax when those strong fingers grabbed his jacket, hoisted him as if he were a weightless straw man and dragged him toward the picture window. He was screaming when he hit the glass and felt it shatter, ripping at his flesh, and then he had no breath to scream with as he reached out with desperate hands to stop the street and sidewalk rushing toward his face.

10

Milan, Italy

Pietro Abandando lit his first cigar of the morning, drawing the rich smoke deep into his lungs. He didn't cough as he savored the aroma and the rush of nicotine. He had a young man's constitution, even at the age of sixty-one, and there was no reason why he shouldn't live to be a hundred.

If he wasn't murdered first, of course.

It was a rough-and-tumble business Abandando had selected for himself when he was barely eighteen years of age. The Mafia had no retirement plan, and a majority of its initiated members died before they reached that golden age, in any case. Some fell to natural causes, but most ran out of time and luck when they encountered bullets, bombs, garrotes, stilettos or the devilish *lupara,* firing jagged chunks of lead that left a man in tatters, like a side of beef the dogs had worried raw. Abandando had survived because a combination of intelligence and animal ferocity allowed him to defeat his enemies, detect potential traitors and eliminate the competition in his rise to stand as capo of Milan. He was a man of respect, feared and honored by his neighbors in roughly equal proportions, though he suspected that fear would win out in the end.

And that was fine.

Times changed, and it had turned into a new world from the one Abandando knew when he was growing up, an ur-

chin on the street, whose dark Sicilian blood set him apart from mainlanders. These days, aside from the historic rivalry with the Camorra, there were Chinese to contend with, cruel Colombians—even Russians, as if Abandando didn't have enough to deal with in his golden years. The Chinese Triads were accommodating, for a price. As for the rest...

His car was waiting at the curb, one of Abandando's soldiers nodding at him and opening the back door, while his driver sat behind the wheel. Good boys, these young ones, though he sometimes wished they had the lean and hungry look of his own generation, greater motivation to excel and grind the enemy to dust beneath their feet. Some grew up thinking it would be a world of milk and honey all their lives, no need to fight for what they wanted—or to keep what they already had. Abandando knew the truth, and he was still a soldier, after all these years. The belly, double chin and waddling gait disguised a tiger who was merely resting, still quite capable of killing if the need arose.

This day, though, there should be no need for killing. Skies were blue above him, the cigar was sweet, and he was looking forward to a leisurely day at his favorite café, sipping wine through the long afternoon, consulting those who stopped with hats in hand to cut a deal, ask favors or repay some kindness Abandando had bestowed on them in days gone by.

It was a good life, all in all.

He rarely had to murder anyone these days.

"Good morning, Don Pietro." Young Luigi smiled at him with the proper deference as he spoke, head tilted in the bare suggestion of a bow.

"Luigi. You look—"

The first shot struck Luigi from behind, a clean hit to the head—though *clean* wasn't the best word to describe it, as the young man's skull exploded, spraying Abandando with a mist of blood and brains. He blinked the gore away, recoiling as the almost headless body toppled forward,

sprawling at his feet. The echo of the shot came back at him belatedly from somewhere on the far side of Viale Monza.

Abandando staggered, instinct taking over as he threw himself on the pavement, crawling toward the cover of some nearby shrubbery. It wouldn't stop a rifle bullet, but at least it might confuse the sniper's aim.

The next shot was directed at his car. Abandando heard a crash of glass, but didn't look back to see if young Alfonso was alive or dead behind the wheel. No matter. Abandando meant to save himself at any cost. Young soldiers could be purchased cheaply. It was the capo's job to stay alive and lead his men to victory against the enemy.

Whoever they were.

Abandando tasted dirt, felt prickly bushes scratching at his face and neck. Worming backward, he soon put a stucco wall between himself and the assassin, cool shade masking his retreat.

Now all he had to do was wait for the police.

And think how sweet revenge would be, when it was his turn to retaliate.

MARCEL BOUCHET had pitched in with the pointer to Milan. Surveillance cameras at the Marseilles airport, operated by the Sûreté to watch for fugitives and smugglers, had detected Tu Sheng as he lined up to board the flight from France to northern Italy. The choice was logical when Bolan thought about it: a short flight to friendly territory, where the 14K and Mafia had forged a grim alliance, working hand in hand to keep the drugs and lira flowing, minimize potential bloodshed and advance Beijing's political agenda on the side.

The ruling capo wouldn't understand that part of it, thought Bolan. They were die-hard capitalists, as devoted to free enterprise as any staunch Republican in Washington, D.C. The Mafia had gone to war against the fascists in the 1930s, and then local Communists a decade later, taking

money from the OSS and CIA in turn to help keep Italy allied with the United States and NATO while the cold war heated up in Europe. If the authorities were kind enough to turn a blind eye to narcotics traffic, rank extortion and the like in payment for services rendered, so much the better. Politics made strange bedfellows indeed, and the homegrown Mafia had been sleeping well for generations in its native soil.

The present boss of bosses, based on information drawn from Interpol, was a sixty-four-year-old convicted murderer named Giuseppe Andolini, who divided his time between Rome and Milan. His Triad counterpart and ally, for the past two years or so, was Mao Hahn, a forty-two-year-old import from Hong Kong, operating on a long-term visa that identified him as a scout for restaurants and hotels. The only scouting Hahn had done to date had been on transportation routes for China white, but no one seemed to mind. The fix was in, and it was business as usual in Milan.

Until the Executioner hit town.

He still had hopes of finding Tu Sheng, but there was more at stake in Italy than nailing down one agent of the ChiCom network. Each new stop along the trail, from San Francisco to Milan, convinced Mack Bolan that his adversary's grand design meant more than simply moving drugs or smuggling Chinese aliens from one point to another, raking in the cash that came from contraband in any form. Beijing cared nothing for narcotics, even less for fugitives—unless the two outlawed commodities were harnessed in some way to serve the People's Revolution. In that case . . .

The picture was emerging piece by piece, and he could guess at much of what had yet to be revealed. The trade in China white was highly lucrative, allowing ChiCom plotters to reduce their own expense accounts and maybe turn a profit on subversion, while the traffic undermined morale and morals in the West. Illegal aliens were flocking out of

China all the time; why not include some spies or saboteurs among the frightened refugees and let them burrow deep in their adopted homelands, ready to emerge and strike on order when the time was ripe? While they were at it, it was no great trick to funnel Chinese weapons and explosives through the Triad pipeline, arming "revolutionaries" from the urban battlefields of Western Europe to the jungles of Peru, Colombia, Thailand and the Philippines.

There were some pieces missing from the puzzle yet, but Bolan saw enough to let him know that he was dealing with an international conspiracy that made the Medellín cartel look like a bunch of juvenile delinquents stealing hubcaps on a Sunday afternoon. Since Russia and her Eastern European satellites had fallen into disarray, Red China was the bloody, beating heart of global communism, as committed to repression of her people and the export of her brutal revolution as she ever had been under Mao Tse-tung or Chou En-lai.

The more things changed, the more they stayed the same.

It could be said of Bolan, too, those words of wisdom from another time and place. His stern commitment to eradicating human predators was carved in stone, a debt he owed himself and those who had already sacrificed themselves on his behalf to stem the dark, malignant tide before it swept humanity away. He cherished no illusions that one man could do the job alone, but someone had to try, and Bolan did the best he could.

Getting by with a little help from his friends.

This day Milan was on the hit list, and the games had just begun. Before the sun went down, this peaceful city in the heart of Lombardy would see a very different side of life—and death.

The Executioner was ready.

KATZ DIDN'T SPEAK Italian, but he had the look to carry off the next phase of his mission in Milan. His gray hair,

weathered skin, even the two-inch knife scar on the left side of his neck would help him pass for Mafia when he came up against the Triad in Milan, as long as none of them invited him to stick around and have a friendly chat.

No problem there, with the Beretta Model 12S submachine gun tucked beneath his raincoat, Katzenelenbogen thought. He had selected an Italian weapon, just in case survivors noticed or he had to leave it near the scene. It was a small thing, window dressing, but he always strove for accuracy. The Beretta semiautomatic holstered under his right armpit made it unanimous, along with the Italian clothes and shoes he wore.

The Chinese restaurant was two blocks west of Milan's Palazzo di Brera. Katz couldn't read the sign in Italian or Cantonese, but it made no difference. He knew exactly where he was, and who was waiting for him once he made his way inside.

The restaurant was one of several businesses controlled by Mao Hahn, the Triad red pole in Milan. He kept an office there, though it wasn't his central headquarters, and Katz didn't expect to find Hahn on the premises this morning. It would be enough to meet with his lieutenants, shake them up a bit and point a guilty finger at the local Mafia.

The sun was warm on Katz's shoulders as he crossed the street, avoiding traffic, but a cool breeze dried the perspiration on his forehead. He was sweating like a rookie, Katz acknowledged, angry at the notion that a simple hit-and-run would put his nerves on edge. It happened to the best of them, of course, but Katz had always felt immortal, even when he lost his arm in action in the Sinai.

A survivor.

Lately, though...

He shrugged away the brooding train of thought and concentrated on his mission. Almost to the front doors of the restaurant, he took a firm grip on the compact SMG,

making sure the safety switch was off before he walked inside.

It wasn't open for business yet, but a custodian was sweeping up the dining room, while waiters dressed in white shirts over pressed black trousers set the tables, laying out the silverware and napkins. Katz wondered idly if they did a decent business in a city like Milan, but it was simply mental small talk. By the time he finished with the restaurant, it would require extensive renovation and repairs.

One of the waiters moved to intercept him, speaking in Italian, but the gruff Israeli silenced him with graveyard eyes, brushed past him and headed toward the private office in the rear. He didn't know the floor plan, but the business part of any restaurant was always tucked away somewhere, kept out of sight. It was a firm, unwritten rule, immutable as any law of physics in the universe.

He passed the kitchen, felt his mouth begin to water at the smell of chicken, pork and vegetables in preparation for the lunchtime crowd. Katz tried to picture dozens of Italians sitting down to Chinese food and quickly gave it up. In front of him, a red door marked Privato held his full attention.

He didn't try the knob, as his hand and metal claw were already filled with hardware. Rearing back to give the door a solid kick, he slammed it open, swinging hard against the wall on the Israeli's left. In front of him, a chubby, balding Chinese with gold-rimmed spectacles was gaping at him.

Two younger men were standing by the desk on either side, and while their faces also registered surprise, they didn't let the sight of Katz's gun immobilize them. Instead, they broke in opposite directions, reaching for the pistols worn beneath their stylish jackets, trying to defend themselves and maybe save the older man behind the desk.

The shooter on his left was closer, quicker, hence more dangerous, and Katz dealt with him first, a short burst to his chest the last word in their grim, one-sided argument. Explosive impact hurled the Chinese gunman back against a

nearby file cabinet, toppling books and papers to the floor, where he came down on top of them and smeared them with his blood.

On Katz's right the second gunner had his pistol out, but he was slow to find his target, fumbling with the safety catch before he got it right. Too late. The short Beretta SMG spit half a dozen rounds and nailed him to the wall, arms splayed to simulate a crucifixion, sliding to the floor and leaving crimson tracks behind him as he went.

And that left one.

The man behind the desk had given up on breathing. He was turning colors, scarlet darkening to purple, and his eyes bugged out behind the glasses as if pressure from within were on the point of detonation. Katz helped out with four rounds from his SMG, deflating him, the tall chair and its occupant punched backward in a clumsy sprawl that took the dead man out of sight.

Back through the dining room, he half expected opposition, but the way was clear. The waiters made a point of keeping eyes averted as he passed, like statues frozen where they stood. Katz tucked his weapon out of sight before he hit the street and barged into traffic, dodging cars and listening to horns bleat wordless insults as he crossed the boulevard.

He was fumbling in his pocket for the car keys when he realized his hand was shaking. Damn! A simple job, and he was trembling like a novice on his first time out.

Nerves were part of living, Katz told himself, and any soldier without feelings was a man just waiting for the ax to fall. Still, he had done this kind of work at least a hundred times before, and he couldn't remember trembling this way since his teens, the first time he went into battle.

Shake it off!

Indeed, he had no other choice. The battle had been joined, and there was no place for him on the sidelines. It

was do-or-die, and Katzenelenbogen only knew one way to go.

Straight down the middle, all the way to the end of the line.

Macao

THE WEEK HAD GONE from bad to worse, and there was still no end in sight for Cheung Kuo. His operation had been shattered by the unnamed enemy in France; police and Corsican thugs were mopping up the survivors, leaving no stone unturned, while Tu Sheng took off for Italy to save himself. And now, as if on cue, the violence had begun once more, this time around Milan.

Coincidence? Was someone stalking Sheng, or could there be another explanation for the long string of disasters they had suffered in the past eight days? It was without a doubt the longest, most depressing week of Kuo's adult life, and he was desperate for a scapegoat, someone who would take the blame, absorb some savage punishment and thereby put his roiling mind at ease.

The trouble was, he trusted Sheng—or had until his agent demonstrated something close to supernatural success in cheating death, while those around him fell like stalks of grain before the reaper's scythe. Was it dumb luck, a show of skill... or something more?

Before the past week's violence, Kuo wouldn't have believed that Sheng possessed the raw imagination necessary to present a risk of treachery. Most any man could stab you in the back, of course, but the rewards involved were often petty—what the crass Americans called "peanuts." It required a fair degree of intelligence, plus certain training, to devise a scheme that threatened countries and empires, and the Dragon had been scrupulous in choosing agents for the field who lacked those qualities.

Or so he thought.

It wouldn't hurt to take a closer look at Sheng, but time was of the essence now. The violent setbacks they had suffered in America and Europe could be fatal to the program if the Dragon didn't seize control, assert himself and do what he did best—whip his subordinates and lackeys into line, make sure they understood the penalty for failure in an unforgiving world.

Sheng would thank him for the stern reminder if he was a loyal agent of the cause. If not, well, it was late to look for a replacement, but removal of a traitor always ranked among the top priorities of any plan. It would be awkward, trying to replace the man who represented Cheung Kuo's apparat in all of Western Europe, but it could be done.

No man was indispensable.

Except, perhaps, the Dragon.

He was still no closer to discovering the names and number of his enemies, though Kuo had nearly convinced himself the men had to be American—their leadership, at any rate. The Yanks had ample reason to despise him—those who knew of his existence, anyway—but would they move against him so aggressively in these times, when their watchdog Congress made a show of counting pennies and avoiding hasty foreign entanglements?

It seemed unlikely. Still...

Someone was stepping on his plans, and Kuo was furious that they had managed to survive this long, harassing him across two continents, five separate countries.

Make that six, with Italy.

His eyes were chips of flint as he reached out to grab the telephone. Invading Italy had been a grave mistake for his unknown opponents, Kuo decided. While they didn't know it yet, the move would cost them everything.

Beginning with their lives.

Milan

McCarter's weapon was the Beretta SC-70 rifle with a folding metal stock, the butt extended now and cool against his cheek. The gun measured thirty-seven inches overall, including its built-in grenade launcher, and it weighed a fraction over nine pounds fully loaded with a 30-round box magazine of 5.56 mm rounds. Its cyclic rate of fire approached 650 rounds per minute in full-auto mode, but it was set for semiauto firing, to save on ammunition and provide for greater accuracy at his chosen range of sixty yards.

The trucks were lined up like a herd of fat, domesticated dinosaurs, all waiting for the master to arrive and fill their feeding trough. In fact, McCarter knew, these beasts of burden had been fed already, diesel tanks topped off, and while he couldn't see the fumes escaping from their tall exhaust pipes, he could hear the engines rumbling even from a distance, seven giant hearts that never missed a beat.

Fanducci's trucking company was known to specialize in contraband, all kinds, no load too dirty or too hot. In years gone by, the big green trucks had carried everything from uncut opium and stolen cigarettes to women, drugged and shackled, headed for the docks in Rome or Naples, where they would be shipped to brothels in the Middle East and Africa.

No human cargo was on board today, according to McCarter's information. He wasn't required to pull his punches out of fear that he would kill or injure any innocent bystanders at the scene. The drivers, for their part, were hard-core Mafia, armed to the teeth against the chance that some demented idiot would try to rob Don Giuseppe Andolini's trucks.

They had to have laughed at that sometimes, the very notion of a hijacking. Don Andolini was the strongest capo on the mainland, his control of sundry rackets guaranteed by fear and favors. No one had the nerve to trifle with his operations, but it helped to make a show of force regard-

less. Andolini had a fearsome reputation to preserve, and it was only wise to maintain strong defenses, even in a time of peace.

McCarter took one of the 40 mm MECAR rifle grenades from his satchel, fitting it carefully over the SC-70's muzzle. The range was perfect, as were the targets. Even if he missed one truck, with seven lined up in a row, it should be no great challenge to produce a killing hit. And once the fireworks started, he was on his way.

He counted sixteen men around the trucks. Assuming they used two-man crews, that left a couple for the chores of maintenance and fueling. Some of them were bound to spot him, even with broad daylight helping to hide his muzzle-flashes, but it didn't matter. By the time they managed to coordinate an armed response, he would be raining death upon their heads; there would be no realistic chance for them to save themselves.

McCarter chose his target, starting in the middle of the line, where an explosion would produce the best results. He took his time and aimed for the windshield, knowing his grenade would drop a bit before it reached the target. That should place it more or less dead center on the big truck's grille, and it would detonate with force enough to crack the engine block, spill burning fuel, perhaps touch off the diesel tanks.

From there it should be easy: take advantage of the first confusion, laying down a screen of killing fire and leaving havoc in his wake when he pulled back, a phantom who spread death and paranoia in the opposition's ranks.

He sighted down the barrel, took a breath and held it, then squeezed the trigger gently with his index finger. The grenade took off downrange, struck home on target with a smoky thunderclap. Within a heartbeat red-and-yellow flames were pooled beneath the stricken vehicle and spreading to its neighbors, while the mafiosi on the ground began to scramble, trying to discover what was going on.

He mounted a second grenade, winged it toward the end of the line on his left and watched another truck go up in flames. The Briton let fly with one to his right, boxing them in with burning hulks, flames spreading rapidly to reach the other trucks.

The crews were scrambling in a hectic bid to salvage something from the holocaust, men leaping through the smoke and flames to mount their loft cabs, throw engines into gear and put the still-undamaged trucks in motion. Starting on his left, McCarter shot one driver through the windshield of his cab, two 5.56 mm bullets in the face and chest that killed him where he sat and left him slumped across the steering wheel. A third round stalled the engine, and his truck was going nowhere fast.

It was the same with drivers two and three, small deviations in the script, but none of them was bulletproof, none of their vehicles impervious to armor-piercing rounds. McCarter did his job efficiently, without a thought to his assailants as a group of human beings. They were targets, plain and simple, predators who made their living by inflicting misery on others, shipping pain and heartache to the world at large.

And it was time for them to pay.

A handful of survivors, still on foot, had found McCarter—or thought they had. Most of the men had pistols, though one had a compact submachine gun, and they were returning fire with more enthusiasm than precision. Given time, they might succeed in trapping him until police or reinforcements could arrive, but he wasn't prepared to let them have that time.

McCarter switched his rifle to full-auto and strafed his adversaries with a long burst, tracking right to left along their ragged line. They made good targets, with the leaping flames behind them, and he watched them stagger, topple and go down. It was impossible to say which ones were wounded, dead or simply trying to avoid a bullet, and he

didn't care. As long as they were down and out, McCarter had a chance to slip away.

It was a short jog to his waiting car, close by the railroad tracks that formed the northern boundary of the warehouse district. By the time he got there, he had tucked the SC-70 beneath his coat, stock folded, and was ready to secure it in the duffel bag behind the driver's seat. The two remaining MECAR grenades joined the rifle, safely out of sight, and he was rolling in another moment, checking out the pall of smoke that filled his rearview mirror, rising from Fanducci's trucking yard.

Take that, he thought, and smiled. They might as well get used to it.

Because the battle in Milan was just beginning, and the Mafia was on the losing side.

DON GIUSEPPE ANDOLINI felt the warm sun on his face and knew that life was good. The villa outside Corsico, southwest of Milan, was his pride and joy, the olive groves providing shade and income all wrapped up in one. The house was custom-tailored to his needs, with marble floors and furnishings no peasant could have purchased if he saved his wages for a lifetime.

Andolini was a "man with a belly," both in literal and figurative terms. He measured five foot six in elevator heels and tipped the scales at three hundred pounds, but the expression was intended to describe a man whose reputation went before him, earning him respect—or fear—from those he dealt with on a daily basis. Andolini was a man whose bloody hands had crushed the life from individuals and small communities alike; manipulated politicians, judges and policemen; smuggled everything from guns and gold to heroin and human flesh at one time or another in his long career of crime. He was a married man who kept a string of mistresses between Milan and Naples, filling in the odd days of the month with any number of the nubile prostitutes who

recognized him as their lord and master. Andolini was a connoisseur of wine, as well as women, and his favorites came from vineyards that he owned around Salerno and Calabria. The one-time owners of those vineyards had been stubborn men, but one had died at thirty-seven, when his car exploded on a rural highway, and the other saw the wisdom of accommodating Andolini's urge to dabble in the business of producing wine.

So life was good, but there were setbacks all the same. Most recently the violence in Milan had challenged him to keep his wits about him, not go rushing off in fury to declare war on the enemy who seemed most obvious. There would be time enough for that once Andolini had the necessary facts in hand. He had learned something, after all, from years of crushing competition, watching out for traitors at his back.

The lesson was a simple one: be sure of who your adversaries were before you sent them off to hell.

The butler cleared his throat and spoke to Andolini in a soft, respectful tone, informing him the Chinese had arrived. Andolini heaved his bulk out of the chair and went to greet his guests. Two men, the butler said, and while he had expected Mao Hahn to come alone, the capo had nothing to fear from two men as opposed to one. His soldiers would have searched them at the door, and anyone who tried to harm him here at home would be confronted with a dozen guns before the men had a chance to blink.

Andolini didn't know that much about the Chinese. Most of them looked the same to him, and these were no exception: yellow men of less than average height, dressed in expensive suits, their straight black hair slicked down with oil. The one on Andolini's left was Mao Hahn, a forty-something shark whose glowing smile concealed a heart as black as anthracite. Andolini knew Hahn was a big-time killer in his homeland, and respected him for that, but this

was Italy, and the Chinese could not forget who was in charge.

Hahn's companion was a slightly younger man whose predatory features had been polished with a certain superficial charm. Hahn introduced the man as Tu Sheng, a colleague from Macao, and Andolini shook his flaccid hand. They sat and waited for the butler to pour wine and made small talk for the first few minutes. Andolini finally came to the point.

"I don't like all this trouble in Milan," he told his visitors. "My men are getting killed. Some think your people are responsible."

"My soldiers have been killed, as well," Hahn said.

"I know this. It's why you're sipping wine and talking to me now, instead of lying in a hole with fresh dirt on your face."

Hahn kept his plastic smile in place and said, "I'm grateful for your understanding, Don Giuseppe."

Andolini waved the thanks away as if it were a buzzing fly. "What reason could you have for making war against my family?" he asked. "We have a contract, no? We all make money while the truce is in effect. It would be foolish for a man in your position to throw everything away, and I am told that idiots are rare among your people."

"They are nonexistent in my family," Hahn told him, smiling still.

"Our problem, then, is to discover those responsible for the disruptive acts and punish them before they cost our families more money we cannot afford."

"My friend can shed some light on that, I think." Hahn turned to his companion, nodding as a signal for the other man to speak.

Andolini listened while the other told his tale in halting words, nerves threatening to choke him up from time to time. The past four days had seen outbreaks of violence aimed at the Chinese and their associates in London, Am-

sterdam and France. Around Marseilles and Paris, someone had apparently provoked a shooting war between the Corsicans and Triads, with the end result that both sides had been seriously damaged. Andolini was familiar with the recent events in France, though he had logically suspected the Chinese of treachery. Sheng had managed to escape each time, unharmed, and while that smacked of a suspicious circumstance, Andolini was prepared to hold off judgment for a time, until he heard what else the Chinese had to say.

"And they were white men?" he inquired when Sheng had finished. "You believe they were Americans?"

"Yes, sir."

"That's very interesting."

"What shall we do?" Hahn asked.

"The first thing we must do," Andolini told him, putting on a mirthless smile, "is mobilize for total war."

11

The small café was located two blocks south of Milan's Catholic University of the Sacred Heart. Bolan felt a bit out of place, surrounded by students and tourists, but they passed him by without a second glance, mistaking him for a native resident, or—at worst—a well-dressed visitor who seemed to know his way around.

In fact, it wasn't Bolan's first trip to Milan, but he had never visited the city on a pleasure trip, and wondered what it would be like to roam around the streets with camera and guidebook, no guns underneath his coat and no one out to kill him any hour of the day or night if he let his guard down for a moment. It would be strange, he thought, to just relax, go with the flow and act as if he didn't have a worry in the world.

It was a price of living on the edge, that loss of humdrum, "rational" perspective on the world. When a man was braced to die at any time, the world took on a whole new set of colors, smells and sounds: more vibrant and intense than he remembered from his younger days, before he donned a uniform. Was it better? Worse? He couldn't say with any certainty these days.

But it was all he knew, and there could be no turning back.

The man he was about to meet at the café was a senior officer with the Italian security service, a unit created in the 1970s to cope with left-wing terrorism, later expanded to

take the heat from neo-fascists and to spearhead an investigation of the Mafia, when the police and prosecutors started running out of guts. A sort of cross between the FBI and Delta Force, the unit carried out surveillance, gathered facts, then moved against its targets with the kind of force most commonly reserved for hostage situations in the West. It worked, to some extent, but they were years away from ending terrorism in the country, much less stamping out the syndicates that had been growing, planting deep roots in Italian soil for over seven hundred years.

But maybe, if he played his cards right, they would lend a helping hand...or stand aside, at least, and let him do his job without the added burden of police pursuit.

It was a lot to ask, he realized, and the Italians had their pride to think of. They were serious about their war against the Mafia—some of them, anyway—and he would have to walk on eggs, watch out for any inadvertent insults when he made his pitch.

It was late morning, and the café was a shady refuge from the sun outside. The raincoat and the Uzi had been left behind in Bolan's rental car two blocks away. He wore a sleek Beretta Model 92 below his left armpit, in a fast-draw rig, and that would have to do if anything went wrong in the café.

His contact was supposed to have a white carnation in his buttonhole. It was an ancient trick, the ultimate cliché, but it had seemed to fit a sunny morning in Milan. He took two steps across the threshold, then spent a moment checking out the room, while an attractive hostess hovered at his elbow, asking him if she could help.

"*Un attimo,*" he told her. "*Cerco un amico.*"

There, to Bolan's left. The man was still a few years short of middle age, hunched forward with his elbows on the checkered tablecloth and sipping coffee, trying not to stare at Bolan. The carnation pinned to his lapel had wilted

somewhat since he left the office, but it was the only one in sight.

Bolan nodded toward the table, left the hostess at her post as he moved off to greet his "friend." The stranger watched him, one hand slipping underneath the table, probably to find a weapon just in case the meet turned out to be a trap.

Smart thinking. Bolan gave him credit. It was always wise to be prepared when you were dealing with a total stranger and the stakes were life or death.

He stopped two paces from the table, risked a smile and asked, *"Parla inglese?"*

His contact raised an eyebrow and replied, "It wouldn't make much sense for me to be here if I couldn't speak the language." When he got around to smiling, it was calm, reserved. "Why don't you have a seat and tell me what you need?"

KATZ HAD SUGGESTED that they dog the meet to cover Bolan's back, but the Executioner insisted there was too much work to do around Milan before they moved on to another killing ground. Katz wanted to believe that they were making progress, knew the enemy was hurting, but the odds against them were so long that the Israeli found it best to concentrate on the here and now instead of looking too far down the road.

Which brought him to the cluttered alley behind a health club near the Castello Sporzesco. It was a Triad hangout these days, taken over by the Chinese mob a year earlier, when they were branching out with their "legitimate" investments in Milan.

They kept the back door locked, but it was old and could have used some maintenance. Katz used his metal claw and sheared off the doorknob, hearing metal clatter on the floor inside. No dead bolt obstructed his entry. He went in with the short Beretta 12S leading, just in case someone had heard the racket and was coming to investigate.

In fact, he had the dingy hallway to himself. The clanking sound of metal from a room somewhere ahead told Katz the men he sought were working out to keep themselves in shape. Some of the Triad soldiers practiced martial arts, he knew, and many of the younger ones were fitness buffs, but muscles wouldn't save them when he had them in his sights.

Katz moved along the corridor, passed by a shower room with water running in an empty stall, no one in evidence. He kept on going, trailed a reek of perspiration to the gym, where he found half a dozen young Chinese at work on weight machines and stationary bicycles. Two others stood against one wall, towels draped across their shoulders, taking five. Several handguns were in evidence, deposited where the young men could reach them in a hurry, should the need arise.

Like now.

Katz didn't bother calling out to them. There was no point in giving up his edge, with odds of eight to one. He started on his far left, milking short bursts from the submachine gun, three men down before the others started to react and scramble for their weapons.

One shooter vaulted from the stationary bike where he was working up a sweat, sprawling facedown on the floor in his attempt to reach the pistol lying on a nearby chair. Katz didn't let him get there. He squeezed off a burst that met him as he rose and flipped him over on his back, blood spurting from a ring of tightly clustered chest wounds.

That made four, the enemy reduced by half, and Katzenelenbogen kept on firing, sweeping the gymnasium with noise and sudden death. His fifth opponent lobbed a barbell at him, but the projectile fell short, and Katz put three rounds in his adversary's back as he was pivoting to grab a pistol lying on the floor.

Five down and counting.

Two of the remaining three had reached their weapons, while the third appeared to be unarmed. Katz left him for

the moment, concentrating on the two with pistols in their hands. They were firing at him, hasty rounds flung high and wide, but he couldn't afford to let them try again, when they would certainly improve their aim. The SMG laid down a string of parabellum manglers, and the two went down together in a tangled snarl of bloody arms and legs.

The bolt on Katz's gun locked open, signaling an empty magazine, and he was grappling with a fresh replacement when the lone surviving Triad gunner bolted for an exit on his left. Katz snarled a curse and started after him, reloading as he closed the gap. He heard the creaking of a locker door and the rustling sounds of fabric as the shooter scrambled for his weapon, rooting clothes aside.

Katz barged in behind him and found the young man turning back to face him, a shiny autoloader held before him in a firm two-handed grip. The guns went off together, and a bullet whispered past the gruff Israeli's left cheek, nearly close enough to graze him, as he cut the young man down. Another half inch to the left, Katz thought, and it would be *his* body twitching on the concrete floor, blood pooling underneath his shattered skull.

Dumb luck.

He gave the locker room another hasty check, found no one prepared to spring upon him when his back was turned. The Triad soldiers seemed to have a free run of the gym, as no staff was in evidence, and it was just as well. Employees with the fear of Mao Hahn behind them might have felt compelled to make some suicidal gesture, throw their lives away on behalf of men who wouldn't cross the street to spit on them if they were doused with gasoline and set afire. This way was better, cleaner.

No loose ends.

The message would get back to Hahn in any case. Katz went out through the front door, hesitating long enough to let a number of pedestrians examine him before he hiked back to his waiting rental car and drove away. There would

be nothing for police to go on, but an Asian mobster might have reason to suspect his round-eyed "allies" if he thought about it long and hard enough.

There had been nothing on the radio so far about a falling-out between the Triads and the Mafia. Not that he followed everything he heard, by any means, but there should still have been some bulletins by now, announcing incidents that weren't linked to Bolan or the men of Phoenix Force. If their design had backfired somehow...

He'd have to take it easy, wait and see.

There was no point in worrying before he knew if there was trouble in the wind. If they were forced to change the plan for any reason, they would change it.

Simple.

All Katz had to do, meanwhile, was stay alive and keep the heat on his appointed targets. There was nothing to it, really.

It would be as simple, for a man of his abilities, as falling off a cliff.

"VITO FORLANI."

Bolan stuck out his hand, a firm, no-nonsense grip.

"Mike Belasko."

"You're American?"

"Is that important?"

"Not to me," Forlani answered, shrugging off the question. "I was told to meet you and I'm here. Do we have business to discuss?"

"I wouldn't be surprised," Bolan replied. "You know Don Giuseppe Andolini?"

"Who does not?" Forlani's smile was almost mocking now. "He's a celebrity of sorts, you know. Six times indicted, but he never comes to trial. The witnesses against him have a way of disappearing or winding up in shallow graves."

"Sounds typical. I guess you know a Chinese named Mao Hahn?"

Forlani lost his smile at the mention of the red pole's name. "We have not met," he said, "but I'm familiar with the gentleman's accomplishments."

"Including his political agenda?"

"Oh, that. You mean his friendship with Beijing?"

"The very same."

"He has a lapdog by the name of Tu Sheng, a Communist who poses as some minor secretary for the Chinese government. In fact, we think he's been supplying arms and money to the Red Brigades for some time now, to help them stay alive."

"You haven't caught him at it, I suppose?"

Forlani shook his head. "He would have been deported if we had. There are suspicions, passing contacts that are easily explained when we ask questions. Still, the Chinese weapons find their way into Italian hands."

"Who's leading the Brigades these days?" Bolan asked.

"Marco Scialfa, twenty-nine years old, a native of Pescara. He's been hiding underground the past three years. We have him charged with half a dozen murders, several bombings, kidnappings—feel free to take your pick. He executed a policeman in Cosenza seven months ago. We almost had him then, but he was lucky. Left his girlfriend and a couple of his comrades to delay us while he slipped away."

"What happened to the others?"

"Oh, they died."

"The last I heard, Don Andolini was no fan of the Brigades."

Forlani laughed out loud at that. "I should say not. Four years ago they tried to raise some money by the normal methods—kidnapping, extortion, robbery. Some of their people from Salerno grabbed Don Giuseppe's granddaughter and asked for fifty million lira. She was six years old."

"What happened?"

"No one really knows. Myself, I think the kidnappers got nervous, worried what the Mafia would do when they were finally identified. In any case, they shot the girl and left her in a ditch outside Sorrento. There was evidence that she had been . . . abused."

"So Andolini's on the warpath for the Red Brigades?"

"He was," Forlani said. "We counted thirteen dead before year's end, all murdered execution-style with a *lupara,* but his anger must have passed. These days he takes no notice of the Red Brigades, and they are wise enough to keep their distance from his family."

"Suppose they weren't?"

"Pardon?"

"I mean to say, suppose Don Giuseppe got the notion they were after him again. Suppose he found out the Chinese were handing guns and money to the men who killed his granddaughter? The men who want him dead?"

Forlani shook his head. "There would be—how you say?—a hot time in our town this night."

"That's what I'm counting on," Bolan said. "What's your position if a shooting war breaks out?"

"Officially we're sworn to stop it. Public safety is our first concern, of course."

"And unofficially?"

Forlani thought about it for a moment—Triads, mafiosi and the Red Brigades, all at one another's throats. If there was only some way to control the action, keep it from involving innocent civilians . . .

Was it possible? Could this man pull it off?

Forlani thought about the recent news from France, from Amsterdam, from London. Something—someone—had been set loose on the Chinese Triads with a vengeance, and their allies in the nations where they put down roots were also getting burned. It was the closest thing to justice he had seen in years.

Vito Forlani smiled and asked, "What is it that you need from me?"

MCCARTER RECKONED they would have guards posted at the villa, north of town. You didn't leave a capo unprotected when the Family was under fire, and Roman Palmintieri was the second-in-command of Giuseppe Andolini's far-flung Family, identified as heir apparent to the throne when Andolini went to his reward. It stood to reason, therefore, that the Family's number two would take care to prevent himself from being gunned down in his own backyard.

And that was fine.

McCarter didn't really care if he got close to Palmintieri at the moment. Sound and fury were his watchwords, heat the pot to a rolling boil and keep it there, do anything within his power to persuade the local mafiosi they were under siege by the Chinese.

To that end, he had brought a helper with him, even though the man was in no shape to lend a hand in aid of what McCarter planned to do. He was—had been—a lowly runner for the 14K, the kind of gofer they sent out with messages when they were feeling paranoid about the telephone. McCarter had been waiting when he stepped out through the back door of a brothel on Viale Monza, and it was a relatively simple task to stun him with the first punch, snap his neck and dump him in the back seat of McCarter's rented car. They were together now, some eighty yards from the home of Roman Palmintieri, with McCarter peering through the telescopic sight of a Beretta sniper rifle while his mute companion lay beside him, waiting for a chance to play his part.

The Zeiss Divan six-power scope had zoom capability. It put McCarter close enough to count the hairs that sprouted from his target's ears or read the label on the pack of cigarettes protruding from his pocket. Eighty yards wasn't much for the Beretta, with its adjustable bipod and heavy, free-

floating barrel designed to reduce vibration in the interest of better accuracy. No space-age model, this one, but a solid bolt-action piece, chambered in 7.62 mm, with five rounds in the magazine. You couldn't kill off an army with the Beretta sniper, but McCarter would get their attention and then some.

He lifted off the scope and finalized his preparations, lifting the Triad gofer and dragging him into a seated position, with his back against the tree a few feet to McCarter's left. It would be close enough, all things considered. By the time the mafiosi finished pumping bullets into him, they wouldn't know if he was standing on his head or swinging from a chandelier when they arrived.

McCarter went back to his rifle, found the sentries on their beat and sighted on the taller of them, counting down the doomsday numbers in his mind. On *one,* he stroked the trigger and watched his man go down as if a giant fist had smashed him in the face, blood spattering the man still on his feet.

But not for long.

His second round ripped into the survivor and knocked him sprawling, just as someone shouted from the house to find out what was going on. A third man showed himself, then ducked back as McCarter made a point of missing him by several inches.

He was standing clearly visible against the skyline by the time four gunners spilled into the yard. He dropped the lead pair, then ducked as their companions opened fire without much hope of scoring at the given range. McCarter dropped his empty rifle and sprinted for the car, well out of sight from Palmintieri's villa, running for his life.

The Briton had the driver's window down, and he sat listening for several seconds, the ignition key in hand. They took no chances, coming up the hill and opening up with everything they had. He didn't bother counting, but guessed

a hundred rounds had been unloaded before the shooting tapered off.

McCarter let the compact coast downhill a hundred yards or so before he switched on the engine. It caught immediately, and he aimed the rental back toward town.

So far so good, but he had work to do. It was too early to relax and hope the players would continue on their own. They needed help, and it would be McCarter's job—along with Katz—to see that they had every opportunity to screw themselves.

An autopsy would indicate the Triad soldier's cause of death, assuming no one shot his head completely off, but in the circumstances, it didn't seem likely that Don Andolini and his troops would be consulting with the local coroner. Their marriage of convenience with the Triads had been tenuous at best, the merger of disparate cultures aggravated by the fact that all concerned were ruthless predators and masters of deception. Trust didn't enter into the arrangement, and with any luck at all, the treaty was about to blow sky-high.

In which case, McCarter thought, he, Katz and Bolan would be standing by to put on the final touches, mop up the ones who tried to get away.

And after that?

McCarter frowned and concentrated on his driving.

Telling fortunes was a skill for gypsies, not for former SAS commandos.

Tomorrow would have to take care of itself.

12

The Palazzo Cristallo was Don Giuseppe Andolini's pride and joy. One of the most exclusive nightclubs in Milan, it catered to the kind of wealthy businessmen and socialites whose ranks would normally be closed to one of Andolini's reputed background. It gave him access to the upper crust, both as their host and as a kind of grudging equal—where his income was concerned, if nothing else. The Crystal Palace let Andolini crack a social barrier that had infuriated him from childhood, seemingly impervious to his achievements as a leader of the omnipotent Honored Society.

Too bad for Giuseppe, Bolan thought, that the Palazzo would be going out of business in the next few minutes. If it didn't break the capo's heart, at least the move was bound to anger him.

And Bolan had it calculated for the Red Brigades to catch the blame.

The pamphlets Bolan carried in the inside pocket of his lightweight overcoat were genuine Red Brigade handouts, with the clenched-fist logo, printed in red and black ink on the cheapest paper available. Vito Forlani had supplied the props, along with several names and addresses for allies of the revolutionary cadre, but his personal involvement would be limited to sideline operations, doing what he could to keep the troops at bay while Bolan and the men of Phoenix Force whipped up a firestorm in Milan.

It might not work, but they could only try. It was their best shot at dividing the Mafia and the Triads, now that the direct approach had failed to bring immediate results.

He had to give Don Andolini credit, likewise Mao Hahn, for holding it together in adversity. They had agreed somehow to wait and see what happened in Milan, and it had worked...at first. McCarter's razzle-dazzle with the Chinese sniper would have Andolini thinking twice by now, and once the Red Brigades jumped in—or seemed to—it would take one very stable capo mafioso to restrain himself from waging all-out war against the 14K.

The club wouldn't be open for a few more hours, but the day shift had arrived to clean, set up the tables, get things started in the kitchen. Bolan came in off the street as if he owned the place, not waiting for an invitation, brushing past the first custodian who asked if he could be of some assistance. When the second moved to intercept him, Bolan asked to see the manager, his hit-and-miss Italian serving well enough so far.

The office door stood open, half a dozen men in shiny suits collected in the hallway, smoking cigarettes and laughing at some private joke. One of them glimpsed the new arrival just as Bolan drew the Uzi from underneath his coat, a warning cry alerting his companions.

A couple of them dodged back toward the office and slammed the door behind them, leaving four to face the Executioner as he cut loose from twenty feet away. They died without a chance to reach their pistols, going down together in a heap, blood spattered on the stucco walls and pooling on the floor.

He stepped around them, stood to one side of the bullet-punctured office door and prepared to kick it in. A pistol shot rang out, immediately followed by two more, the bullets missing Bolan by a yard as they punched through the door around chest level.

He responded with a burst that nearly sawed the door in two, reloaded swiftly and went through the doorway in a diving shoulder roll. He came up firing, caught one mafioso as he tried to duck below the Uzi's line of fire, and stitched a line of gushing holes across his chest.

The lone survivor dropped his pistol, raised both hands and started babbling pleas for mercy. Bolan stroked the Uzi's trigger and cut the whiner's legs from under him, leaving him sprawling in his own blood, head and shoulders braced against the wall. He would survive if someone called the paramedics soon enough, and in the meantime Bolan left a little something for his reading pleasure to distract him from his shattered knees.

The revolutionary pamphlets made a trail behind him as he stalked out of the club. It was so obvious, a child could spot the ruse, but that was one advantage when it came to working with political extremists of the left or right. They favored melodrama, sweeping gestures to impress their public, and they mouthed the kind of simple-minded nonsense normally reserved for comic books and TV situation comedies. Above all else, they loved to sign their acts of violence with a flourish, taking credit for atrocities as if the very act of spilling blood would somehow validate their empty lives.

Don Giuseppe Andolini would believe, because it was the kind of mindless stunt the Red Brigades would pull, *had* pulled on numerous occasions in the past.

And with a bit of luck, it just might be the spark required to light the powder keg.

DON GIUSEPPE ANDOLINI slammed the telephone receiver into its cradle, leaned back in his chair, then reached out with a meaty fist and struck the silent instrument once more. In olden times it had been customary for a nobleman to kill the messenger who brought bad news, but Andolini didn't have that option in the present day.

His men were dying fast enough already.

The Red Brigades, dammit! After all this time, the pain they had inflicted on his family once before—and the grim punishment they had received as a result—would they be fools enough to start another war that they were bound to lose?

Why not?

Where zealots were concerned, common sense went out the window. Men abandoned all pretense of rationality and sacrificed themselves, their loved ones, total strangers for the cause. It made no difference if their gesture was a waste of time; the main thing was to keep your name and cause before the public eye, exciting anger, sympathy, disgust—for as long as possible.

The worst thing, though, was knowing that his age-old enemies were armed and financed by his so-called friends, the same Chinese who swore they had no part in the attacks on Andolini's soldiers in Milan throughout the morning. He had wanted to believe the words of Mao Hahn, maintain the truce to mutual advantage, but the truth was coming home to Andolini now: a Chinese sniper killed while taking shots at Roman Palmintieri's villa; pamphlets from the Red Brigades—a group that claimed an estimated two-thirds of its funding from Beijing—found at the Crystal Palace, where another five of Andolini's people had been killed. The sole survivor vowed that his attacker was Italian—not Chinese, at any rate—but Andolini didn't care whose finger pulled the trigger.

He was looking for the man who gave the orders.

Mao Hahn.

The Red Brigades would have to suffer, too, of course. He had been generous the last time, stopping after thirteen of the so-called revolutionaries had been executed to avenge his grandchild's murder. Anyone with common sense would certainly have learned his lesson, but a zealot was incapable of logic.

And if the zealots nursed some grudge against Don Andolini from their last encounter, brooding over his reaction to the violence they themselves had foolishly initiated, well, he had no doubt that they would bide their time, consult their Chinese sponsors and derive a plan of action tailored to serve both at once.

The Triads were insane if they believed they could replace the Mafia in Italy, or even operate on equal terms. Their reputation for ferocity meant nothing to a man like Giuseppe Andolini, who had cut his teeth on murder and extortion from the time he was an adolescent.

If Mao Hahn was looking for a war, he'd get one. All his talk of unity and friendship came to nothing, when the bullets started flying and his lackeys, bought and paid for, were the men behind the guns.

Andolini had restrained himself so far, with difficulty, but the time for self-restraint was past. He would retaliate at once, in strength, against the Triads and the Red Brigades. He'd teach them both a lesson this time, a lesson that would linger in the minds of the survivors and their children's children if they ever thought of making such a stupid move again.

His treaty with the 14K had been a money-maker, granted, but he saw it now for what it really was: a kind of Trojan horse, persuading him to let the Chinese set up shop in territory they couldn't have hoped to seize by force. Once they were well established in Milan and elsewhere, Hahn had seen his chance to strike from ambush, stab his "good friends" in the back and claim an empire for himself.

But he had failed.

Perhaps if he had executed Giuseppe Andolini at the start, there would have been some hope for victory. But the Chinese had missed their chance, and they would pay for that mistake.

In blood.

THE SMALL APARTMENT on Viale Tomba had been fingered as a hangout for the Red Brigades. Not quite a safehouse, it was known to the police, and therefore shunned by active fugitives from justice. But the revolutionaries kept a mimeograph machine and other office hardware on the premises, hacked out their ranting broadsides there and watched the place in shifts against the day when "fascist pigs" would try to round them up and send them to concentration camps in Sicily.

The paranoid delusion gave them focus, but it didn't help to prepare them for the stark reality of Yakov Katzenelenbogen in the flesh.

He rode up in the elevator, clutching his Beretta SMG and wondering how many soldiers would be waiting for him when he disembarked on four. Scratch that. They might be killers, but they weren't *soldiers,* any of them. Soldiering meant discipline, and there was nothing in the background of the Red Brigades to demonstrate that they possessed that quality to any degree. They were prepared to kill and maim, of course; some of them were undoubtedly prepared to die. But they had been seduced by a romantic fantasy revolution, dating from the sixties, when it was enough to grab a gun or hand grenade and learn a catchy slogan.

Power to the people!

Freedom now!

They were naive and immature, but no less dangerous for all of that. With backing from the Red Chinese, they could fight on for years, perhaps for decades. Crushing some of them before they killed again would be a public service.

Katz stepped out of the elevator and turned left, moving toward the door marked 413. Someone's unlucky number, but the revolutionary ethos of the Red Brigades had no more truck with superstition than it did with the Judeo-Christian value system.

There were no guards posted in the hallway, so he had a clear shot at the door. Katz took a short step backward,

brought his right foot up and put his weight behind the kick, his heel impacting just beside the doorknob. The lock snapped off, opening the way for what became a headlong rush. Young, startled faces—one of them a woman's—were turned in his direction as he entered, the Beretta Model 12S held in front of him and seeking targets as he crossed the threshold.

Part of Katz's mind was counting heads and logging four—no, there was number five, emerging from a bedroom at the rear—before he started firing. Short bursts from the SMG conserved ammunition as his targets scrambled to reach weapons they had stashed at various strategic points around the flat.

A tall young man with hair that fell to his shoulders grabbed a pistol from its place beside the mimeograph machine, then turned back to face his adversary as a burst of parabellum manglers opened up his chest. He took the printer with him when he toppled over backward, man and his machine dashed into ruin on the threadbare carpeting.

The terrorist emerging from the bedroom had a pistol in his hand. He pegged a shot at Katz, but he was hasty and forgot to aim. The bullet passed a foot or so above the Israeli's head, and Katz's aim was better with the submachine gun, stitching holes across the revolutionary's naked chest. He staggered backward, reeling, and collapsed across the threshold of the bedroom, motionless.

The woman attacked while Katz was lining up his next shot at her male companions, coming at him with a pair of scissors in her fist, held daggerlike and slashing toward his face. The claw that was his right hand caught her wrist, clamped tightly, and he heard bones snapping as he twisted, shook the scissors free and thrust her from him.

Three men remained, and one of them was diving toward a doorway on the right. Katz helped the runner reach his destination with a short burst in the back, his target levitat-

ing with the force of impact, slamming head-on into a collision with the door frame.

That left two, and both of them were holding pistols as Katz confronted them. The nearer gunner fired a shot that stung his shoulder, but the fleeting pain told Katz it was a flesh wound. He replied with half a dozen parabellum rounds at point-blank range, a disemboweling burst that spun his target like a cutout figure in a sideshow shooting gallery before it left him draped across the sofa.

Katz dropped to a crouch as the surviving terrorist cut loose, shots echoing in the cramped apartment. He was running low on ammunition, but there was still enough to drop one adversary if he did it right.

There had to be.

He felt a bullet tug at his sleeve, another whisper past his ear. Katz zeroed in on target and held down the submachine gun's trigger, the last rounds of the magazine dropping the young man in his tracks.

The small apartment smelled of blood and cordite. Katz was backing toward the open door, about to reload the Beretta, when the young woman he had disarmed a moment earlier returned to the attack. She shrieked and cursed him in Italian, clawing at his face with her good hand. She had no weapon this time, but her rage almost made up for the deficiency.

Katz swung the SMG with everything he had, connected on the right side of her skull and dropped her senseless at his feet. He reckoned the police would have some pointed questions for her, and she might wind up in jail, but it had been her choice from the beginning. Personal responsibility was part of growing up, and it applied to revolutionaries just the same as anybody else.

He walked back to the elevator, feeding the Beretta as he went. There was no need to leave a message for the leaders of the Red Brigades. They would assume the worst, and when the net began to close about them, Bolan and Mc-

Carter hauling in loose ends, the logical conclusion would be an assault by soldiers from the Andolini Family.

And it was all downhill from there.

Like sliding on a laundry chute to hell.

MARCO SCIALFA HAD BEEN twelve years in the revolution game, most of that time in various positions with the Red Brigades. He knew the way things worked, how old mistakes sometimes came back to haunt you at the worst of times. He hadn't been involved in the abduction of Don Giuseppe Andolini's grandchild some years earlier, but he wasn't above such tactics if they helped promote the cause. He recognized the old-line Mafia as one more tool of fascist domination in his homeland, and he preached to his disciples of the day when every trace of capitalism and slavery would be swept away.

So far, regrettably, the revolution had been faltering. In fact, it had come close to a complete collapse two years earlier, between insistent pressure from the Mafia and apathy among the generation that he counted on for new recruits. Momentum from the seventies and early eighties had begun to peter out, attrition thinning out the ranks. Scialfa's personality alone had saved the movement from extinction, breathing new life into tired ideals and prompting fresh new faces to enlist. The numbers still weren't great, but they were getting better, and he had a whole campaign mapped out, complete with incidents that would ensure fresh headlines, thereby drawing in more recruits.

In the scenarios he planned, however, it was always men and women of the Red Brigades who did the killing—either gloriously, in broad daylight, or by stealth—to rid Italy of fascist hangers-on who should have been eliminated years earlier. Not one of his ideas included unknown gunmen shooting up their safehouse on the Viale Tomba, leaving four men dead, and one woman in the hospital with a concussion and a fractured wrist.

What did it mean?

Scialfa didn't have to ponder that for long. From Lena's brief description of the shooter, smuggled to Scialfa by a sympathetic nurse while the police were on a coffee break, he guessed that Don Giuseppe Andolini was responsible for the attack. The old man would be carrying a mortal grudge against the Red Brigades until he died, and now it seemed that he was having trouble with the Chinese in Milan, some of the very men who kept Scialfa's operation solvent with their cash donations and a steady flow of military hardware.

It was the wrong time for a showdown with the Mafia, but there appeared to be no choice. Scialfa couldn't hide and pray for peace while Andolini's soldiers ran amok and killed his men. Such a response would be interpreted as cowardice by his disciples, jeopardizing his control of the Brigades, perhaps his very life.

No, he would have to fight, and hope for some assistance from the Chinese who had put him in this grim position to begin with. It was their fault, more than anyone's, that Andolini had renewed his blood vendetta with the Red Brigades. Why else would he let three years pass before he struck again?

It still wasn't too late, Scialfa thought. Andolini would be on his guard, but there were ways to make the old man drop his guard, get close enough to strike a killing blow and settle this once and for all. The secret lay in stealth and misdirection, drawing Andolini's eye away from the approach his killer would adopt. No problem, with the wealth of targets that Scialfa had to choose from in Milan.

But he would have to start at once, while he had men enough to pull it off. Any delay at this point could be fatal to his plans.

Scialfa was prepared to sacrifice himself in the pursuit of revolution, but he hoped to choose the time and place, if that was possible. A bullet in the back from some old mus-

tache pete wasn't his notion of a proper revolutionary's death.

When that day came, he meant to have a giant captive audience. It would be glorious.

And he would be remembered until the end of time.

DAVID MCCARTER LAY PRONE on the sunbaked rooftop, sweating through his clothes and watching shadow figures move inside a fifth-floor apartment across the street. Below him traffic flowed along Viale Morbillo, pedestrians thick on the sidewalks. They would have to watch themselves, McCarter thought, but if he played his cards right, there should be no major injuries below.

Unless something went wrong.

He shouldered the Beretta SC-70, the built-in launcher fitted with a long MECAR grenade. It ought to be an easy shot, no more than fifty feet, the kind of shot you made in training without a hitch.

The apartment was yet another bolt-hole for the Red Brigades. He wasn't sure how many of the half-baked revolutionaries were inside; there had been no time for a census while he was preparing for the strike. Some women, possibly, but that wouldn't dissuade McCarter from proceeding with his plan. Each member of the left-wing cadre took an oath to kill and terrorize his or her fellow citizens in the pursuit of "revolutionary justice," and the ones who hadn't pulled a trigger yet were still responsible for hiding fugitives, transporting weapons and explosives to the front-line killers, helping keep the terroristic juggernaut in motion.

Sympathy was the last thing on McCarter's mind.

The small apartment had a balcony, perhaps twelve feet across and six or seven deep, with access from the living room through tall glass doors. That made it easy for a sniper on the far side of the street, and with the MECAR rounds,

McCarter didn't even have to scope specific targets. All he had to do was sight and squeeze.

Beginning now.

The tall glass doors were perfect. Even closed, they offered no significant resistance to the 40 mm round. It should explode well back, inside the living room. The second round would have no obstacle at all, and anything beyond that would be mopping up before he fled the scene.

It would be more than enough to let the self-styled urban warriors know someone was thinking of them, keeping them in mind.

He watched another man-size shadow move across his field of fire, from left to right, and disappear into the tiny kitchen cubicle. Tightening his finger on the rifle's trigger, he inhaled, released a portion of the breath and held the rest.

The first grenade went in on target, shattering the glass door near its center, detonating three-quarters of a second later, smoke and thunder rolling out across the patio. McCarter slipped a second MECAR round onto the launcher, found his mark and fired again into the churning smoke cloud.

McCarter hesitated, on the verge of pouring 5.56 mm rounds into the shattered flat, then let it go. If someone managed to survive the conflagration, he or she would carry word back to the leaders of their cadre—and the word would spread, regardless, even if nobody walked away.

He closed the rifle's folding stock and slid the weapon back inside its olive drab duffel bag. The service elevator took him to the street, and there was nothing to it, mingling with the awed pedestrians who stood and pointed, gaping at the cloud of smoke emerging from the gutted apartment above. No one took any notice of McCarter as he turned away and walked back to the nearby parking lot, where he had left his car.

Experience had taught him that your average urban revolutionary had a personality combining equal parts of egomania and paranoia. A direct assault of this sort punched the panic buttons on both fronts, outraging any targets who survived, inflaming their desire for swift revenge, while heightening the sense that everyone was out to get them, traitors lurking everywhere with daggers poised to strike at unprotected backs.

Around Milan, if Bolan's theory was correct, the Red Brigades would instantly suspect Don Giuseppe Andolini of initiating the attacks, and once that link was made, they would feel honor-bound to pay him back in kind.

More fireworks, then, and he would be around, with Katz and Bolan, to mop up on the survivors.

It was dirty work but someone had to do it before the savages had time to mount a winning play.

THE AIRWAVES TOLD the story, Bolan's scanner picking up police calls as the action heated up. He didn't follow everything they said, but there were names, addresses, details he could pick out of the cross talk, telling him that the campaign was still on schedule, moving toward what he hoped would be a final detonation in the next few hours. By the time the sun came up the following morning, there would be some fundamental changes in Milan.

With any luck at all, the good guys would come out on top.

Vito Forlani had provided more than simple pointers to the Red Brigades. He knew, for instance, that the wily Tu Sheng was hiding out with Mao Hahn at the red pole's estate near Sesto San Giovanni, in the northern suburbs of Milan. Surveillance placed the two men together when they called on Giuseppe Andolini earlier that day, and they had gone back home, lying low from that point on.

It gave the Executioner a target, and his car was pointed northward on Viale Monza while he listened to the scanner

and kept track of flare-ups on the urban battlefield that was Milan: a clash between suspected Red Brigades commandos and a carload of hardmen from the Andolini team; a drive-by shooting at a Chinese gambling club that wasn't on the target list for Phoenix Force; a car bomb detonated in the alley behind a bar where Andolini's soldiers liked to hang around between engagements, drinking wine and talking tough to make themselves feel more like heroes than the human scum they were.

He listened to the numbers, made it twenty-seven dead or wounded in the action he and his colleagues had instigated, nudging one side into conflict with another, turning up the heat. Divide and conquer was a tactic he had used on other battlefields, an opportunity to take advantage of the paranoia that was part of every outlaw's personality.

No matter how often they killed, how many victims they had terrorized, the men who lived on the blood and sweat of others were always watching for the knife thrust from behind, a friend's false smile, the hidden trap. Duplicity was such a part of life that mobsters, terrorists and such suspected there was no one they could trust.

And they were right.

They stayed alive, on top, by using fear against their fellow men—including friends, subordinates and enemies alike. A man who lied, killed and cheated to attain his status knew from the beginning that those waiting in the wings to take his place would use the same techniques, perhaps more ruthlessly than he, if he wasn't on guard against their treachery. The law was out to get him, too, regardless of the bribes he paid and witnesses he silenced in an endless quest for personal security. The only true peace he would ever know was in the grave—assuming hellfire wasn't waiting for him on the other side.

That insecurity, the mental isolation that it fostered in most predatory individuals, could be a lethal weapon in the proper hands. Mack Bolan was a master when it came to the

manipulation of appearances, stage-managing disasters for his enemies. Before they knew it, he could have them hip deep in piranhas, fighting for their lives and wondering exactly how they'd gotten there. If it helped disrupt the very operations he was sworn to interdict, so much the better.

All was fair in love and war, they said, and Bolan's war was dirtier than most.

With any luck he would be finished in Milan within the next few hours. He already had a fair idea of where he would be going next, and by the time he finished mopping up in Italy, the final choice would have been made.

The Executioner reckoned they were somewhere past the halfway point of his campaign against the 14K's unholy merger with Beijing. He had no handle on the men in charge as yet, but he was getting there. The point of no return was well behind him, with Bolan and his allies locked in for a wild ride that would carry them to the end of the line.

The terminal.

But terminal for whom?

He concentrated on his driving, pictured Tu Sheng, and felt his fingers tighten on the steering wheel.

There would be time enough to think about what happened at the finish line when he was closer. Right now he had to focus on the enemy's offensive team and do his best to knock them down.

And this time, if he did it right, Sheng would have no chance to slip away.

13

Marco Scialfa racked the slide on his Beretta semiautomatic pistol, chambering a live round as his driver pushed the Fiat to its limit, weaving in and out of traffic, leaning on his horn. It was the normal style of driving for Milan, and Scialfa wasn't worried by the prospect of police attempting to detain him. Any officer who tried was in for a surprise. Three of his soldiers were crowded in the back with automatic weapons

Behind him, keeping up as best they could, were three more cars, with five guns each. If Scialfa lost them momentarily in traffic, it would make no difference. The drivers knew where they were going; each of them had driven past Don Andolini's villa and knew exactly where to find him when he was at home.

It wouldn't have been Scialfa's choice to fight the Mafia, but Andolini had removed all options with his vicious sneak attacks. Retaliation was demanded, and the more he thought about it, he had convinced himself that taking out the capo would do wonders for morale. Andolini was a symbol of the stinking, rotten system, after all, a parasite who sucked the blood and dreams from working men and women every day. The Red Brigades would have to deal with him sometime, so why not now?

Why not, indeed.

It was an easy run to Corsico, southwest of town, despite the traffic. By the time they reached Andolini's villa, all four

cars were running close together like a caravan. There were no gates on the mafioso's private drive, but guards were always posted, rain or shine, to make sure no one took their capo by surprise.

This night Andolini had four soldiers on guard, a small concession to the violence that had lately rocked Milan. They saw the headlights coming and showed no interest until the lead car swerved directly toward them, dirt and gravel spewing from beneath its tires. Scialfa had his window down, his submachine gun poking out. He held down the trigger and watched one of the mafiosi skitter through a jerky little dance before he fell.

Then everyone was firing, weapons roaring from the back seat, thunder deadening his ears. Scialfa ducked, pure reflex action, as a bullet cracked the windshield, clipped off the rearview mirror and dropped it on the floor beside his foot. He had a brief impression of gunmen rushing forward through the darkness, firing as they came. The villa was ablaze with lights, as if the capo had prepared a welcome party for his uninvited guests.

Scialfa grinned, more snarl than smile, and clutched his weapon tightly, finger curled around the trigger. Gunfire rattled in the night, and bullets struck the Fiat as they raced along the curving driveway.

It would be good to kill him: good publicity, good for the movement, good for Scialfa's soldiers, who could still remember Andolini's massacre of their loyal comrades years before. No matter that Scialfa's predecessor was responsible for that vendetta, picking on the capo's grandchild when he could have stolen any other girl in Italy. There was a principle involved, a debt of blood that had been too long brushed aside.

Scialfa braced himself as a Mercedes-Benz came out of nowhere, charging on a hard collision course to intercept the Fiat. His driver spun the wheel and managed to avoid the worst of the collision, slamming broadside with the Benz.

Behind Scialfa guns were going off, his soldiers laying down a screen of fire as he bailed out and landed on all fours, the Fiat rocking under concentrated gunfire as he scrambled clear.

Keep going!

But he was having second thoughts, as he glanced back at the bullet-punctured car and saw one of his soldiers tumble, lifeless, from the open door in back. The other cars were drawn up in a ragged skirmish line, facing the villa, and Scialfa's comrades piled out, firing in all directions as they found themselves surrounded by the enemy.

How many guns? It had to be roughly even, from the muzzle-flashes he could see. They had a chance at least.

And what choice did he have, when there was nowhere he could hide?

MACK BOLAN WAS about to scale the wall of Mao Hahn's estate when the crew wagons arrived. Three black limos advanced on the gates, ignoring sentries who tried to flag them down, then opened fire with automatic weapons when the point car failed to brake in time.

He used the clamor from the gates as a diversion, dropped into a crouch and struck off toward the house. The sounds of combat would be drawing every Triad soldier on the property, while Bolan had a clear shot at Hahn's villa from the rear.

Good timing. The Executioner wished he could have planned it on his own, but he was satisfied to know that he had set the wheels in motion, whipping up a war between the erstwhile allies. Any damage suffered by the two opposing sides was good news from his point of view.

He was on his own with Hahn and the elusive houseguest, while Katzenelenbogen and McCarter covered the play at Andolini's place in Corsico. Between them, if their luck held out, they should be able to conclude their business in Milan before another sunrise lit the killing fields.

He reached the tree line at the rear of Hahn's estate, prepared to cross thirty yards of open, neatly tended lawn that lay between him and the house. There was a swimming pool to Bolan's left, a tennis court off to his right. The patio in front of him included whitewashed wrought-iron furniture and a new brick barbecue as tall as a fair-size man. Beyond the patio, glass sliding doors gave access to the house, the drapery drawn against the night.

Bolan made his break, was halfway there when movement to his left made him turn in that direction. One of Hahn's protectors had appeared, perhaps attempting to avoid the action that was heating up out front. The soldier gaped at Bolan, raised his submachine gun and was squeezing off a burst when Bolan shot him in the chest.

The 5.56 mm rounds from his Beretta SC-70 drilled tidy holes on impact, tumbling after penetrating flesh to open catastrophic wounds and slam the gunman backward off his feet. He went down kicking, held his death grip on the SMG and fired off half a magazine in the direction of the quarter moon that lit the battleground.

So much for stealth, but there was still a chance that the Executioner could reach the house without concerted opposition from the occupants. Out front it sounded as if a full-pitched battle was in progress, lacking only field artillery to make the scene complete. A few stray shots from the direction of the patio might pass unnoticed if Bolan was lucky.

He kept on going, hardly breaking stride, and made the patio in seconds flat. The sliding doors were locked, and looking for another means of entry would waste too much time. He swung his rifle butt against the glass, reached through to free the latch and slid the fractured door back, almost in a single motion. Curtains whipped around him like a clinging shroud as Bolan charged into the darkened sitting room, a large-screen television on his right, with leather-covered chairs and sofas scattered all around.

He crossed the spacious room in long, swift strides, prepared for any challenge from the enemy. Sheng was somewhere in this house, if Bolan's information was correct, and he had chased the ChiCom agent long enough. It would be all or nothing now, no more false starts and missed connections. Sheng had used up all his luck and then some—but the Executioner still had to find him before he could make the tag.

He was three paces from the door when it flew open, almost in his face, a Triad soldier barging through. The man was responding to the crash of glass perhaps, or on some errand for his master. His mouth dropped open at the sight of Bolan and the automatic rifle, recovering too late to save himself, his shotgun swinging up toward target acquisition as a burst of 5.56 mm tumblers ripped into his chest and throat.

The guy went down, his body wedged against the door to hold it open, like some ghoulish doorstop. Bolan stepped across the corpse and moved along a spacious hallway, following the sounds of combat as he sought his human prey.

MCCARTER HAD INITIALLY resisted Bolan's plan for Katzenelenbogen and himself to watch Don Andolini's villa while Bolan went to face the Triad gunners on his own. There was no point in arguing, and he had done as Bolan asked. Now he was in the middle of a firefight that had all the makings of a battle royal, and he wouldn't have cared to guess the likely winner on a bet.

The Phoenix Force warrior had the north side of the villa covered, lying sheltered in a grove of olive trees, the stock of his Beretta sniper rifle snug against his cheek, the SC-70 beside him, fitted with a 40 mm MECAR round. He scanned the killing ground through his six-power scope, a momentary pause as he reviewed the battle lines.

The Red Brigades assault force had been stopped short of the house, but they were hanging on, the four cars lending

them some cover, like a wagon train besieged by hostile savages. From where he lay, McCarter counted three invaders stretched out lifeless on the ground, but their surviving comrades were returning fire in lively style, with no apparent fear of running low on ammunition. Andolini's troops, meanwhile, were at a disadvantage as they tried to rush the cars across the open lawn. He counted seven mafiosi down and out, a couple of them still alive but obviously fading fast.

McCarter chose a target—one of Andolini's soldiers, crouching on the porch—and framed it in his cross hairs, taking up the trigger slack by slow degrees. The rifle bucked against his shoulder as the 7.62 mm bullet left the barrel at a velocity of some 2,838 feet per second. It lost a bit of steam before it reached the crouching man, but not enough to matter. Through the scope McCarter saw his target lurch, spin like a top and crumple on the deck like so much dirty laundry.

Moving on.

To keep things fair, he chose his next mark from among the Red Brigades attackers. It was tricky with the angle, but he had a partial view between two vehicles and held his sights there, waiting for a likely target to reveal itself.

The gunner was a stocky fellow, and a shallow cut above one eye had smeared the left side of his face with crimson, like a fright mask.

McCarter took the shot before it slipped away from him. His bullet drilled through the young man's chest, a bit off center, but it did the job. He vaulted backward, kicking as he fell, and went limp as he stretched out on the grass.

Three rounds remained in the sniper rifle, and the general confusion of the war in progress covered his more modest efforts fairly well. McCarter's third shot dropped a mafioso on the run as he was trying to approach the young invaders from their blind side, getting close before the bullet plucked him off his feet and dropped him in a heap.

Round four was easy. One of Andolini's men had started firing from an upstairs window, altitude allowing him a different angle of attack, his submachine gun burping 3- and 4-round bursts. McCarter shot him in the face and blew him back out of sight, his weapon slipping through the window as he lost it, clattering across the porch roof and dropping into the yard.

Picking out another target from the Red Brigades assault force, he lined up a head shot, stroked the rifle's trigger and watched his adversary's head explode like a ripe watermelon with a cherry bomb inside.

McCarter laid down the sniper rifle, picked up the SC-70 and peered downrange through open sights. Selection of a target for the 40 mm MECAR round was no great challenge. In a heartbeat he was lined up on the nearest of the vehicles the Red Brigades had used to crash the gate. The Briton held his breath and squeezed the trigger, soaking up the recoil with his shoulder, watching the grenade bore in on target like a guided missile.

When the Fiat blew, it brought a new dimension to the battle—smoke and leaping flames, distorted shadows. The members of the stunned assault force hastily regrouped, their weapons spitting death in all directions. They were scrambling to get clear before the gas tank blew, and most of them would make it. By the time that secondary blast lit up the yard, McCarter had another MECAR rocket mounted on his rifle and was sighting toward the house.

Fair's fair, he thought. He squeezed the trigger, slamming his high-explosive round through one of Andolini's tall front windows, smiling as it detonated in the house and sent a rolling cloud of smoke across the porch.

"All right," he said to no one in particular, "it's party time."

THE FIRST REPORTS of gunfire from outside found Tu Sheng relaxing in the room provided by his host—or trying to, at

any rate. The past few days had made it difficult for him to eat or sleep, except as he imagined fugitives had to do: in haste, without enjoyment of the simple acts that were so crucial to survival. Liquor helped to take the edge off, but he wouldn't let himself indulge beyond the point where he experienced a warm glow in his stomach, since he might be called upon to flee at any moment and would need all his wits about him in the race for life.

Like now.

The sounds of automatic-weapons fire could mean only one thing, as far as Sheng was concerned. His unknown enemies had found him once again, and it was time to run or die.

Run where?

His thoughts had no coherent fix beyond the moment, couldn't focus on tomorrow or the next day, when he might be killed at any moment. He would have to flee the house, go down the back stairs and make his way outside. If he could reach a car, find one with keys in the ignition, he could—

Sheng was moving toward the closet, homing on his suitcase, when the door flew open. Mao Hahn and several of his men intruded on the Communist's solitude. Sheng hesitated, standing in the middle of the room, uncertain what he ought to do or say.

"The damned Italians," Hahn snarled. "They try to kill me now, by treachery."

Sheng had his doubts, but he could see no point in arguing. It made no difference, really, who the gunmen were. He would be just as dead from an Italian bullet as from one made in America.

"What will you do?" Sheng asked his host. The question sounded foolish even as he spoke, but Hahn didn't appear to mind.

"We're getting out," the red pole said. "You come with me."

"My clothes..." He nodded toward the closet.

"There's no time. You can replace those things another day. We have to leave right now."

Sheng bit his lip and nodded like a faithful peasant. "As you say."

At least he had the pistol, tucked into his belt at the small of his back. Its reassuring weight told Sheng that he could still protect himself whatever happened. He wasn't compelled to put his faith in Hahn exclusively. If all else failed—or Hahn tried to betray him somehow—he would use the weapon as a last resort.

And if he came close to being captured, Sheng knew, the Dragon would expect him to reserve one bullet for himself.

No fear of that, however. If the past four days had taught him anything, it was that his persistent enemies didn't take prisoners. They were completely, admirably ruthless when it came to wiping out the targets they selected. Under different circumstances Sheng might have tried to hire them as occasional assassins for the People's Revolution, but that option was beyond him at the present time.

He had to concentrate on getting out of there alive.

Hahn led him from the bedroom toward the very stairs that Sheng had planned to use in making his escape. Another Triad soldier waited for them on the landing, covering the stairs. Out here, it seemed, the sound of gunfire was much louder, closer. Sheng could pick out frightened, angry voices shouting back and forth in Cantonese, Italian, some of them just screaming, wordless cries of agony or rage.

Familiar sounds.

Hahn nodded to his pointman, and the soldier began to lead them down the stairs.

They would clear the house in minutes if they weren't intercepted. Hahn had to have a car on stand-by, some way to get past the enemy out front. The red pole was no idiot; he wouldn't let himself be trapped this easily, with no means of

escape. Perhaps it was a good thing, after all, that Sheng was in his care. A few more yards, and they—

The shock of the explosion hurled him backward, sprawling on the stairs, with Hahn on top of him. A cloud of smoke rolled over Sheng, obscuring his vision, but he didn't need his eyes to know that they were trapped, cut off, with nowhere left to run.

THE RUSH WAS NO SURPRISE to Katz when it began. He knew the Red Brigades attack force would be forced to move once the grenade McCarter fired at them had destroyed a portion of their cover, spewing gasoline and flames around the tenuous perimeter they had established. It didn't have to be a safe move necessarily, but hasty relocation was a must if they intended to survive.

That left them to select a destination, which was basically no choice at all. A run back toward the gate was suicide, a dead-end gauntlet past a score of automatic weapons, nothing at the other end except for miles of open road and hostile countryside. If anyone survived the dash, it would mean being stranded in a ritzy neighborhood of Corsico, while mafiosi and police fanned out to comb the streets for stragglers.

It was the house or nothing, and the odds were terrible in either case. The strike team had to be having second thoughts by now, but it was too late to reconsider their position. Pride and anger had delivered them to this grim pass, and they would have to make the most of it.

They made the move, some kind of flying wedge. Not bad, all things considered, even taking hits the way they were. Katz saw one of the runners stumble, go down on his hands and knees, his weapon lost. He tried to rise, but blood was soaking through his sweater in the front. His strength went with it, and he finally slumped forward on his face.

By that time his companions had abandoned him in their rush toward the villa, firing on the run. Katz gave them

credit as they cleared a handful of surviving mafiosi from the porch, a couple of them moving toward the broad front door as it swung open to disgorge Andolini's backup team.

Too much to hope for, Katz decided, that the don would show himself. This kind of killing was a young man's work. The thought made Katzenelenbogen hesitate, but he was in the middle of it now, no turning back.

Another of McCarter's MECAR rounds sizzled in to smash a second window, detonating in the capo's living room. The blast took out a couple of Mafia gunmen, just emerging through the door, but otherwise it made no lasting difference to the battle on the porch. It wasn't easy, fighting hand to hand with SMGs and pistols; there was no room to maneuver, and was a challenge even aiming when your adversaries were all over you.

A bit like Sinai and the battle where Katz lost his arm.

To hell with that.

He started moving in, no mindless rush, but getting there. The nearest mafiosi didn't see him coming, had their first suggestion of a problem when he opened up with the Beretta 12S from behind them, almost kissing-close, and chopped them down like targets on a shooting range.

He kept on going, spent the last rounds in his magazine on two more gunners, pivoting to face him on his right. Katz hosed them with a stream of parabellum manglers and watched them fall, reloading as he turned back toward the house.

McCarter had him covered, firing another 40 mm grenade that blitzed a Fiat in the middle of the yard, its detonation giving Katz some clearance, hammering a pair of Andolini's gunmen to the deck.

The action on the porch was nearly finished when he got there, dead and dying soldiers sprawled together, some still clutching one another, frozen where they fell. The stench of death and cordite made Katz want to vomit, but he swal-

lowed hard and started breathing through his mouth to beat the old, familiar smell.

Somebody struggled upright on his left, blood smeared and wobbly on his feet. Katz shot him in the chest, three rounds to finish it, and didn't wait to watch him fall. In front of him the door stood open, lazy tentacles of smoke reaching out to feel their way across the porch.

Katz glanced back at the trees, where his companion would be covering his flank. He glimpsed a muzzle-flash, saw one of Andolini's people stagger and sprawl on the grass. The time for hesitation was well behind him now as Katz turned back to face the doorway, stepped across the threshold, fanning with his metal claw to dissipate the smoky haze.

Don Giuseppe Andolini stood before him in the rubble, looking like a sleepwalker awakened in the middle of a dream. No injuries were visible, though Andolini's face was smudged with soot, his gray hair rumpled, standing out in spikes. The capo had a shiny automatic pistol in his hand, but it was pointed at the floor. He stared at Katzenelenbogen, blinking rapidly, as if to clear his vision and his thoughts.

Katz shot him where he stood, the parabellum shockers punching Andolini over on his back.

It was that simple at the end, and Katz wasn't inclined to wait around to find out if Andolini had more soldiers hiding somewhere in the house. Their work in Corsico was done, and it was time to leave.

He flagged McCarter, who was coming through the smoke across the porch, and started jogging toward the trees. Behind him somewhere, someone had begun to holler for Ansielmo, sounding frantic when there was no answer.

Katzenelenbogen left him to it, thankful for the silent darkness that was waiting for him in among the trees. McCarter found him halfway to the car and fell in step.

"Are you all right?" he asked.

"I'm fine," Katz said.

And knew that he was lying even as he spoke.

BOLAN'S 40 MM MECAR round exploded five steps from the bottom of the staircase, spewing fire and shrapnel as it detonated, flattening the five men on the stairs. It could have been enough, with luck, but thrashing movement and the sound of angry voices told him that his work wasn't completed.

He couldn't tell if Andolini's men were gaining ground out front, but there had been no letup in the sound of automatic weapons blasting from the villa's porch and yard. How long before a frightened neighbor summoned the police? They could be on their way by now, he realized, and knew that he was running out of time.

But he couldn't leave yet, not with the prize in front of him.

There had been time for him to recognize Tu Sheng and Mao Hahn before he dropped the bomb on their parade, the pointman swallowed up in smoke and thunder as he died. A couple of the others might be wounded, but it didn't seem to hamper them as they scrambled to their hands and knees, then stood, bent on finding cover or returning fire.

Two soldiers brought up the rear with submachine guns, dazed but holding it together, unloading fire toward the room below them, laying down a screen of cover fire for Hahn and his companion. Bolan hit the deck and rolled behind a large recliner, pulling in his legs to cheat the Triad soldiers of their target. They were firing at him, all the same, with the recliner taking hits. He heard the bullets ripping into leather and padding, making little zinging sounds when they found metal springs.

He had to keep them occupied somehow if he couldn't take them out immediately. Pinned behind the chair, he had no chance at Sheng or Hahn. They could escape, and he would be back where he started, scrounging for a break.

Bolan palmed another MECAR round and mounted it, the rifle's muzzle heavy with the weight of the grenade. He wasn't able to aim with great precision, but he took a chance, leaned out around the side of the recliner and let fly in the direction of the stairs, above where he had placed the first grenade.

He didn't see the grenade detonate, but its concussion rocked the chair where he was hiding, and the submachine guns momentarily fell silent. Bolan saw his opportunity and didn't hesitate. He emerged from his meager sanctuary, tracking with the SC-70 as smoke rolled down the stairs.

Tu Sheng was kneeling, one arm thrown across the banister to hold himself upright, his free hand wrapped around some kind of semiautomatic pistol. Mao Hahn, beside him, was a pale face peering through the smoke and sifting plaster dust. His soldiers were alive but stunned or wounded by the latest blast, their movements awkward, jerky.

Bolan rose and took a long stride toward the stairs. He saw Sheng's automatic rising and fired a burst that punched the ChiCom agent backward, flat against the wall. A second burst satisfied him that it was done.

Hahn was struggling to his feet, apparently unarmed, but coming empty-handed to the battle wouldn't save the red pole's life. Another burst of 5.56 mm bullets knocked him sprawling, tumbling down the stairs like some failed acrobat who needed more work on his routine.

Too late.

The soldiers were a write-off. Dead or simply dazed, they were no threat to Bolan now. He left them squirming on the stairs and backtracked through the house, the same way he had come. A portion of his mind was following the sounds of outside combat, but they seemed distant and unreal, much like the sound track of a movie playing in another room.

He thought of Katzenelenbogen and McCarter, wondered if they would be waiting for him at the rendezvous. No

problem if he had to hang around awhile and drink some coffee. That way he would be alert and wide-awake when they proceeded to the airport, moving on.

The battle had been won, but there was still a war ahead of them, with enemies who weren't aware of his existence.

The Executioner would have to introduce himself, and soon.

Despite a measure of fatigue, he found that he was looking forward to it.

14

Rangoon

The government of Burma discouraged casual tourism. Perpetual rebellions by the Shan and Kachin factions, raging for the past three decades, were embarrassing to the Rangoon administration and a hazard to the uninitiated wandering through would-be combat zones, a prime consideration in the state's decision that no casual visitor could remain in the country for more than a week.

No problem, McCarter thought as he traveled west on Anawrahta Road, approaching Chinatown. If he and his companions were in Burma a week from now, they would be dead, their mission passed to other hands.

Despite the march of time and endless civil war, Rangoon still had a flavor reminiscent of an Asian capital from the 1940s, with beautiful tree-lined streets fanning out from the center of town, quiet residential districts interspersed with lakes and half-hidden valleys. Around the Turf Club, the World Peace Pagoda, along Embassy Row, the casual observer might almost imagine he had stumbled through a time warp to a kinder, gentler era, before rampant crime, terrorism and wars of "national liberation" had emerged as the scourge of the Third World.

Forget the history, McCarter told himself. There was a mission to complete.

The 14K had put down roots in Burma fifty years earlier, when leaders of the clan began to see which way the wind was blowing in their native China, with the Communist rebellion gaining steam and battering the right-wing Kuomintang. Another practical consideration was the proximity of what the world had learned to call the Golden Triangle, that acreage in Burma, Laos and Thailand—not to mention China's Yunnan Province—where a clique of feudal warlords kept their private armies, raising poppies for their opium, refining it to China white for sale abroad.

The red pole in Burma was a stone-cold killer known as Chik Fu. It might have been the handle he was born with, but at the moment McCarter neither knew nor cared. The *man* would be his target, when it came to that, not the persona he adopted for his public.

Fu's contact in the Triangle was Tuan Khoo, described by DEA as number two among the several warlords operating in the region. Khoo had at least three thousand soldiers in his personal militia, theoretically devoted to eliminating communism from their homeland. They were more concerned, in fact, with moving opium and heroin across the border into Thailand, where it found its way to Bangkok and the thriving markets there.

Ironically, while Fu was a nominal conservative, and Khoo stood somewhere to the right of Heinrich Himmler, Fu had also played along in 14K's collaboration with Beijing. According to the CIA and other sources, ChiCom arms and cash provided most of the support for a left-wing guerrilla army in the northern provinces of Burma, led by one Maung Win, a die-hard "liberation warrior" from the same school that produced the Vietcong and Khmer Rouge.

Strange bedfellows, McCarter thought as he arrived outside the Chinese gambling club on Anawrahta Road.

A trench coat would have been incongruous in the oppressive heat, with humidity approaching ninety-five percent. The lightweight sport coat was a burden in itself, but

necessary to conceal the mini-Uzi slung beneath his right arm on a swivel mount, the Browning double-action automatic sheathed below his left.

He breezed in through the double doors, chilled by a rush of welcome air-conditioning. The smiling hostess might have been eighteen, but he wouldn't have cared to bet on it. McCarter asked to see the manager, and while she seemed to understand his halting Cantonese, the young woman hesitated—until he let her see the SMG.

"Come this way," she said, and turned her back on him.

He fell in step behind her, keeping one hand on the Uzi underneath his jacket.

AUDACITY DROVE Bolan to the high-rise office block on Merchant Street. All things were relative, of course, and "high rise" in Rangoon meant twelve to fifteen stories, as opposed to some of the impressive skyscrapers in Bangkok, Hong Kong and Kuala Lumpur. Still, it was tall enough to make escaping from the penthouse office suite a problem if Bolan hung around too long and let the troops assemble below him, cutting off his access to the street.

Timing was everything, a fact of life as true in warfare as in stand-up comedy. Blow one pursuit, and you were red faced when the audience declined to laugh; screw up the other, and they needed dental charts to verify who you had been.

He rode up in the elevator, wondering if Yuan Chan would be available. The second-in-command for Chik Fu's Burma family, Chan was a pencil pusher who had graduated from the ranks of common muscle on the basis of initiative and brains that went beyond the average. He still used certified accountants to maintain the books, but Chan kept tabs on every Triad shipment entering or leaving Burma, whether it was uncut opium or China white, munitions for the rebels, children for the Patpong district in Bangkok or

women headed for the brothels of Luzon, Manila, Seoul or Taipei.

Chan had his manicured fingers in a score of rotten pies, and he wouldn't be missed by any of the thousands he had victimized. His passing *would* be mourned within the 14K, however; it might even start a panic if the Executioner got lucky.

There was no time like the present to find out.

He had considered silencing the Uzi, but then decided it would be a waste of effort once the home team started shooting back. His time on-site was limited in either case, and he had weighted down his belt with frag grenades at the last minute, just to help the odds along.

Two sentries lounged in the hallway as he left the elevator, frowning at the stranger, straightening to face him with expressions on their faces that were probably rehearsed, attempting to convey a mix of menace and determination. Their leather jackets were unbuttoned so that they could reach their weapons in a hurry if they had to.

Bolan didn't give them time, the Uzi blasting even as he brought it into view. A stream of parabellum slugs ripped through his targets, dropped them writhing on the carpet.

The Executioner passed by them, the sound of startled voices drawing him toward his targets. A young woman poked her head out through the first door on his right, then ducked back at the sight of Bolan's weapon. But the door stayed open, and he shouldered through it, sweeping with the SMG, dismissing the woman as she darted out of sight behind her desk, no weapon in evidence.

A rough-looking man emerged from the door of a private office on the right, his thousand-dollar suit and fifty-dollar haircut unable to hide the legacy of murder in his eyes. He snapped at Bolan, wasted noise in Cantonese, and raised the pistol that he carried flush against his thigh. The Uzi stuttered, caught him in the chest with a 4-round burst

of parabellum tumblers and put him down before he had a chance to fire.

The dead man wasn't Chan, but Bolan reckoned he was getting closer to his man. The next gunner who showed himself was leveling a shotgun by the time he cleared the doorway, this one to the left, and Bolan ducked below the blast of buckshot that didn't have time to spread from fifteen feet away. He answered with a short burst from the Uzi, but his target had retreated out of range.

The frag grenade felt warm and heavy in his palm. He pulled the pin and lobbed the bomb with a sidearm motion, bounced it off the jamb and through the open doorway to the office on his left. A startled voice cried out before the blast eclipsed all other sound and filled the corridor with swirling smoke.

It was the only cover he could count on, and he took advantage of the moment, moving forward in a crouch, the Uzi leading. He heard some kind of scuffling sounds in the last office, dead ahead, but had no way of knowing who it was or whether Chan was behind that door.

There was only one way to find out.

He rushed the door and bulled through it, dropping to the floor inside as bullets rattled overhead. He had a glimpse of two men standing and one hunched behind a massive desk, all three with handguns blasting from a range of twenty feet or less.

He held down the Uzi's trigger and swept the room with bullets, watching the two lean gunners jerking, reeling, going down, while their companion dropped completely out of sight. A ringing silence settled on the room, and Bolan took advantage of the lull to change positions, rolling several paces to his left.

And none too soon.

The man behind the desk—Chan, no doubt about it this time—came erect with two guns in his hands, unloading toward the spot where Bolan had been lying prone a moment

earlier. Too late the red pole understood his critical mistake and tried to swing around and pick up his target, but the SMG caught him halfway there and punched him backward, stumbling as he fell against his high-backed swivel chair, then dropped to the floor.

Chan was alive when Bolan reached him, but the light was fading fast behind his dull brown eyes. There seemed to be no point in conversation, since his time was running short, and there was no good reason to believe the dying man would understand him anyway.

He left Chan leaking blood on the floor, watching out for any stray survivors as he put the suite of offices behind him. Things were heating up around Rangoon, but they still wouldn't reach the boiling point for some time yet.

They had been lucky so far, blitzing through the Triad capitals of Europe, but in Asia they were closer to the center of the web, a dark, malignant spider waiting for them as they homed relentlessly on Hong Kong and Macao. Resistance would be more determined here, worse yet as they drew closer to the hub of the empire, but he saw no other way to do the job.

The Executioner was blitzing on... but not without a measure of assistance from his friends.

IT WAS DIFFICULT to picture any warlord setting up a business office, but the second-story space on Strand Road was exactly that. Tuan Khoo was known to sell the great bulk of his product through the 14K, but he had other customers, as well. The Yakuza sent men to parley in Rangoon from time to time, as did the Filipinos, South Koreans and a certain fat man from Djakarta. It wasn't unheard-of for Americans to make the journey, but they typically preferred to deal with Khoo from a distance when they could.

Such was not the case with Yakov Katzenelenbogen. He was fond of working close whenever possible. There was less

chasing after targets that way, if you had them covered going in. At his age...

What? Katz caught himself in the middle of a weird, one-sided argument. What about his age?

He shrugged it off and stared across the street. A few blocks north and west, the vast Bogyoke Market would be teeming with the usual mix of Burmese residents and foreigners, all bent on finding bargains on a panoply of merchandise that ranged from native arts and crafts to fruit and vegetables. He crossed the street against light traffic and approached his target from the west.

The name of the establishment was unknown to Katz, but he had the address memorized. If there was any doubt, the guard who lounged around out front dispelled it in a heartbeat as he reached for a pack of cigarettes in the breast pocket of his shirt, his jacket disarranged enough that Katz could see a pistol hanging underneath his arm.

The Israeli tried a friendly smile as he approached the shooter, knowing it would get him nowhere. When the lookout challenged him in curt Burmese, Katz kept the smile turned in place and started fumbling in his jacket pocket with his left hand, doing his impression of a hapless tourist who'd misplaced his phrase book. As the gunman was about to speak again, Katz lashed out with his right arm, smashed the metal claw into his adversary's larynx. He followed the first blow with a shove that drove his man into the recessed doorway.

It was over in a flash. A sharp knee to the groin, then he had a crushing grip around the shooter's head and a swift twist with weight behind it finished the job. The dead man settled on his backside, slumped into a corner of the alcove with his head thrown back, mouth open, like a sleepy drunk.

Katz found the Uzi with his left hand, brought it out and double-checked the safety. Satisfied that it would rock and roll upon command, he pushed on through the door—no windows or surveillance cameras here—and climbed a flight

of dingy stairs to reach the office he was seeking. He barged through the door without a knock or invitation, covering the young man at the desk as he went in.

It took about three seconds for the frozen scene to fall apart. The desk man gave a squawk, shoved backward in his chair and tried to reach some kind of weapon stashed beneath his coat. Katz shot him in the chest, four parabellum rounds at point-blank range, and kept on moving as the lifeless body slithered to the floor.

There would be no drugs on the premises, of course. Khoo wasn't an idiot. His people might take orders here, negotiate a price for bulk deliveries, but they wouldn't risk wearing out their welcome in conservative Rangoon. A payoff to Burmese officials only went so far, in terms of nailing down protection. Criminals, regardless of their wealth and status, were expected to obey some basic rules of conduct in the city, and dispensing heroin from walk-up offices was definitely not included on the short list of approved activities.

Katz knew he wouldn't find Khoo around the office, either. When the warlord visited Rangoon, no more than once or twice a year, he took the best suite at the Inya Lake Hotel and stayed for three or four days tops, while business was completed with his underlings. Khoo didn't linger in the city, preferring the security of his established stronghold in the jungle, some two hundred miles due east of Mandalay.

For now Katz would be satisfied to send a message back and rock the warlord's world a bit.

Two soldiers moved to intercept him, firing on full-auto as they came. Katz dodged behind a bank of metal file cabinets, reaching out left-handed to unleash a long burst of his own. One of the guns was silenced, and he heard a satisfying thump as someone hit the floor. The other gunman ducked and started to retreat, still firing, but his options were limited.

Katz palmed a frag grenade and pitched it sidearm, dodging back as angry bullets rattled off the file cabinet, flaying paint. He started counting down the seconds, got as far as three when the grenade went off like thunder in the claustrophobic corridor.

A glance around the corner showed him one man stretched out on his face, blood pooled beneath him, the other near the back wall of the smallish office suite. The second shooter was alive, but only just. His shrapnel wounds were deep and numerous, all bleeding freely, draining him of life. His weapon had gone missing in the blast somehow, but Katz was cautious as he closed the gap between them.

They were alone, from all appearances. The doors that yawned on either side of Katz led into empty office cubicles, with vacant desks and silent telephones. There was no toilet, and he guessed that tenants of the floor were forced to use a public rest room somewhere close at hand.

In any case he found no cubbyholes where an assassin could conceal himself. Katz stood above the dying gunman for another moment, wishing there was something he could say, aware before the thought took shape that he had no real message for this man, no wisdom to impart. Their paths had crossed, and one of them was on his way to hell.

Case closed.

And yet it didn't seem to be enough somehow.

Katz put the killing room behind him and backtracked to the stairs. Another moment put him on the street, and he was grateful for a breath of air that smelled like flowers rather than the reek of blood and cordite.

Getting old, he thought.

But not done yet.

Katz had a war to finish, and there was no room for doubt or second thoughts. His enemies were evil, and they had to be destroyed.

The only question in his mind right now was whether he could do the job.

SO FAR SO GOOD, Bolan thought. They were right on time, and he was rolling toward a one-on-one with a potential ally in Rangoon. Not government this time, but a reformer who had been referred to Hal Brognola and the team at Stony Man by someone in the CIA. With any luck at all, the man wouldn't turn out to be some starry-eyed idealist who spent his free time writing pamphlets on the advent of Utopia.

He passed the Shwe Dragon Pagoda, driving north in the direction of the university. He had the name and address of a café near the university, where he was told his contact would be waiting for him on the stroke of noon. If he was late, the meet was canceled automatically, and there would be no second chance.

No sweat.

He still had half an hour free and clear, and he was almost there. It gave him time to think about the risk that he and his companions had assumed when they left Europe, carrying their battle to the very streets and jungles where the 14K was strongest, with a long-established history of operating unopposed. When wars were fought about the drug trade in the Golden Triangle, it was one Triad vying with another for control. Outsiders rarely got this far, and while the Executioner had been up-country once or twice himself to teach the drug lords fear, he understood that it was no walk in the park. Battalions could be lost without a trace in that vast jungle; three men wouldn't even make a ripple when they disappeared.

But they were not just *any* men. His own experience, from Vietnam and later wars, might be enough to see them through, and his companions were the cream of the elite divisions in their native countries, honed to razor sharpness in a thousand life-or-death collisions with the enemy. If they were lost somewhere "out there," it wouldn't be for lack of

skill or training, much less from a shortage of determination to succeed. None of them was immortal, granted, but they had survived this long, and he could almost see the finish line from where he stood.

Or maybe not.

The Triangle was part of it, of course, but it wasn't the end. To shut down the pipeline, they still had three more major stops, and they would have to find the men responsible for setting up the network in the first place if they meant to wipe it out once and for all. His last check-in with Stony Man had yielded nothing new in that regard, and Bolan wondered what would happen if they came this far, through all that blood, and still couldn't locate their enemy.

What then?

Forget about it.

He was used to taking one step at a time, allowing the momentum of a given action to produce results that might be unexpected from the outset. Wait and see what wriggled out into the daylight when you flipped that mossy stone or opened up that basement door.

Life had a way of dishing up surprises, sure, and while they were unpleasant sometimes, that was simply... life.

And it was better than the grim alternative.

It was embarrassing to call upon his hill chief in regard to matters he would normally have settled by himself, but Chik Fu felt that he had no choice. The sudden violence in Rangoon appeared to fit the pattern seen in Europe recently, and red poles everywhere had been commanded to report if anything unusual should happen in their territories, anything that might in some way jeopardize the 14K's arrangement with Beijing. There was a difference between the time zones, but he couldn't help that, either. If his master was disturbed, so be it.

The scrambler on his private telephone was a concession to technology. The Burmese government had given Fu no major difficulties since he started paying certain ministers and law enforcement officers to look the other way. He didn't furnish drugs to Burmese addicts, and the gaming halls he operated in the heart of Chinatown served only the Chinese. When it was necessary to eliminate competitors, Fu was discreet. He made them disappear, as if their mothers never gave them birth, and everyone was satisfied—except perhaps the dead.

And who were they?

He tapped out the number from memory, twelve digits with the country code, and waited as another telephone began to ring in Hong Kong. It was answered on the third ring by a voice he didn't recognize. It didn't matter. When Fu

gave his code name, he was put on hold for thirty seconds while his master was retrieved and summoned to the phone.

"*Wi.*" This time he knew the voice. There could be no mistaking Edward Wong.

"Discretion is advised," Fu told his hill chief, and engaged the scrambler without saying more. His master would do likewise, and the conversation—while it sounded normal to Fu—would be incomprehensible to anyone eavesdropping on the line.

"You have some information to report?" Wong wasted no time on amenities.

"I have."

"Proceed."

Fu told him everything, such as it was: the flurry of attacks his men had suffered in Rangoon, and the raid on Tuan Khoo's office, which was almost certainly connected to the other incidents, despite a lack of solid evidence. When he had finished, there was silence for a moment on the other end. Wong took his time, considering what he was told.

At last he said, "You must rely on Tuan Khoo. He has an army at his beck and call."

"Five hundred miles away," Fu told his hill chief, trying not to contradict or argue.

"Then your enemy must be encouraged to relocate," Wong replied.

"I have not yet identified the men responsible," Fu explained.

"It makes no difference. They desire your death. We know this from events in North America and Europe, do we not?"

"Yes, sir."

"Then you must go where they are bound to follow. Do not fail. I will communicate with Tuan Khoo soon. He will be ready, waiting for you."

Fu didn't entirely like the sound of that, but it wasn't his place to disagree. An order from the hill chief had to be carried out at any cost.

"It shall be done," he said.

"I knew that we could count on you. Goodbye."

The line went dead, his scrambler disconnecting automatically once there was no one on the other end. Fu cradled the receiver, frowning as he thought about what he had to do.

It meant a trip into the jungle, into peril, with his life in Tuan Khoo's hands. The warlord was a friend, of sorts—at least where business was concerned. And yet...

"It shall be done."

Speaking to the empty room, Fu had a sudden, helpless feeling that wasn't at all his style. Accustomed to control, he felt that he was being swept along by forces and events he didn't understand.

The red pole wasn't frightened yet, but he was getting there.

THE CONTACT'S NAME was Sein Salong. He was an ex-policeman, with a military background, who had pulled the pin on law enforcement in Rangoon when he discovered that the Triads had a fix in with the state.

Or so he said.

It was the background Stony Man received from Langley and relayed to Bolan when he asked about potential Burmese allies, but he knew enough to watch out for himself, taking nothing at face value. Sein Salong would have to prove himself before the Executioner was ready to entrust his life—much less the lives of his two comrades—to a total stranger.

The only other white man in the small café sat in a corner by himself and kept his head down, studying a newspaper. The suit he wore looked as though it doubled for pajamas and hadn't been pressed in several weeks. The other

patrons, thirty-five or so, were all Burmese, Chinese or Indian. The hostess acted as if she was expecting Bolan, flashed him a smile and led him to a table occupied by a Burmese of thirty-something years. His smile was welcoming and cautious all at once.

"I'm Sein Salong," the Burmese said in English.

"Mike Belasko."

"Please, sit down."

He sat and spent another moment checking out the other patrons, watching out for anyone who showed excessive interest in a new arrival.

"We are safe here," Salong informed him.

"If you say so."

"You don't trust me yet. Of course, I understand."

"It's nothing personal."

"But simply common sense. Self-preservation, is it not?"

"You could say that."

"Indeed. Allow me to establish—how you say?—my bona fides?"

"That's what we say."

"I was a soldier for my country, fought against the rebels in the north for six long years. When that was done—for me, at least—I came back home to work as a policeman in Rangoon. I thought to help my country one way or another, yes?"

"Sounds good to me."

"And me...except some people in the government, for all their talk of morals and preserving our historical traditions, are more interested in building fortunes for themselves."

"I've heard we have a few of those in Washington," Bolan said, smiling at the man who faced him from across the table.

"These men want no crime in Rangoon's streets—none visible to them, at least—but they don't seem to care if Burma is used as a way station for narcotics moving on to

Bangkok and the West. They take bribes from the Triads and become rich men, uncaring what effect their treason may have on the country."

"That's not why I'm here," Bolan said, hoping it was clear that he wasn't in Burma to attack the state regime.

"I understand. You seek to crush the 14K, I think...and maybe their connection with Beijing?"

"You're getting warm."

"How better to protect my country?" Salong inquired. "The Triads once were anti-Communist, at least. Today their dealings with the Red Chinese promote rebellion in Burma, with appalling loss of life. They must be stopped. If nothing else, an interruption of their tribute payments to the government may give some good men time to think about their souls. As for the bad men, maybe they will get fed up and find another line of work."

"You really think so?"

"At the moment it's my only hope."

"We'd best get busy, then," Bolan said.

"Yes, indeed. You've come for Chik Fu, I understand."

"He's one name on the list."

"You will not find him in Rangoon. He's run away. Perhaps an hour ago, no more than two."

"Run where?"

Salong smiled. "To hide with Tuan Khoo. You recognize the name?"

"It rings a bell."

"His name is on your list as well, perhaps?"

"I'd like to meet him," Bolan said.

"And I can help you."

"Oh? How's that?"

"I know the region," Salong informed him. "I was stationed there in military service. I can guide you."

Bolan hesitated, checking out the pros and cons. They clearly needed help to find Tuan Khoo, but he had met this stranger only moments earlier, and trust was hard to come

by in the hellgrounds. Even if Salong was all he claimed to be—unselfish, dedicated to his country—there was the moral problem of involving a civilian in the action, where he stood a decent chance of getting killed.

"If I say yes?"

"We leave this afternoon," Salong said. "As soon as we collect the necessary articles."

"You understand the stakes?" Bolan asked.

"Ah, you mean the risks?"

"Whatever. There's at least a sixty-forty chance the other side may take you out if come with me. On the flip side, if you try to set me up, you've got no chance at all."

"I readily accept your terms," Salong replied. "If there is nothing else . . . ?"

"Not off the top," Bolan said, hesitating for another moment, finally reaching out across the table for his would-be ally's hand. "We understand each other, then."

"Indeed we do. Death to our enemies."

"I have a feeling," Bolan told him, "that there'll be enough to go around."

Hong Kong

WHENEVER EDWARD WONG approached the Dragon, even with good news, he felt a certain tightness in his chest, the vague suggestion of anxiety that harked back to his childhood, when he still felt fleeting pangs of guilt at stealing from the Hong Kong market stalls. It wasn't guilt this time, however, but a hint of fear, and all the more humiliating for that private knowledge.

Why was he afraid? The Dragon needed him, his soldiers and his network. That had been made clear a thousand times, and still Wong felt a nagging sense of apprehension every time they met. He knew the Communists, the way they operated, stabbing one another in the back at every opportunity and calling it a bold stride forward for the People's

Revolution. Wong could understand that kind of politics, had lived with much the same conditions in the Triad all his adult life, but this was different, somehow. He had cast his lot with lifelong enemies, accepted their assurance that his empire wouldn't be endangered—would indeed enjoy vast benefits—if he agreed to help them. And it had gone smoothly for a time, no problems . . . until last week.

Within the past nine days, though, nearly half his red poles—*all* of the important ones in North America and Europe—had been killed, their forces decimated, crucial trade routes jeopardized or utterly disrupted by a faceless enemy. The situation was intolerable, and the news was only getting worse.

Which brought Wong to his present, most distasteful chore.

He had to tell the Dragon what was happening in Burma. It was even money Cheung Kuo already knew about the violence in Rangoon from sources of his own, but Wong was obligated to inform him, and he would lose face—at least—if he didn't fulfill his duty. Still, Wong thought that he had dealt with the situation adequately, all things considered. When their adversaries clashed with Tuan Khoo's three thousand soldiers on the warlord's home ground, it would be very different from a hit-and-run engagement in the city, where police ran interference for both sides.

It was another world out in the jungle, hopefully the last one Wong's elusive enemies would ever see.

He dialed the Dragon's cutout number and waited while the call was shunted to another line. Wong's scrambler was engaged, the switching station in Macao one more precaution to evade detection by British or Portuguese authorities.

"Yes." The Dragon's voice was soft, low pitched, a cultured tone. He could have been a radio announcer if he cared to work, instead of plotting revolution for a living.

"I have news," Wong said.

"I'm listening."

"There have been several incidents around Rangoon. Attacks on Chik Fu primarily. Tuan Khoo lost several men, as well, in one attack."

"Is it related to our European problem?" the Dragon asked.

"I assume so. It is better to be safe."

"Indeed."

"Our dealings with the Yakuza have all been peaceful for the past twelve months at least. The other Triads may be jealous, but they would not challenge us—much less Tuan Khoo—in such a way."

"I trust your judgment, Wong."

But did he really? It was something he could say and change his mind five minutes later, turn on Wong as if he were an enemy. You couldn't be too careful with the Dragon; Edward Wong had seen that for himself, first-hand.

"I've taken steps to end this foolishness in Burma," Wong informed his business partner from Beijing. "I don't want these accursed round-eyes getting any closer to Hong Kong."

"What steps?" the Dragon asked. Was that a trace of dark suspicion in his tone? Did Kuo question Wong's ability to handle problems in the field?

"I'm sending them to meet Khoo," he said almost defiantly.

"Explain, please."

"Chik Fu has left Rangoon on my instructions, taking no pains to conceal his movements. Anyone who really wants to follow him will find a way. Tuan Khoo will have a warm reception waiting for them, if and when the round-eyes get that far."

There was dead silence on the line for several moments, while the Dragon thought about Wong's plan. At last his

mellow voice said, "It's a good plan. You're to be congratulated."

If it worked, he meant, Wong thought, but kept it to himself. If he succeeded, Kuo would be pleased to share the credit, tell his masters in Beijing that it was *his* idea. Conversely if the plan should fail, it would be Wong's concept from start to finish; *he* would take the heat alone and wear the mark of failure like a crimson blemish on his face.

Which simply meant that he could not allow the plan to fail. He had to impress upon Khoo and Fu the urgency, the absolute necessity of wiping out their enemies in Burma, where they had at least a fighting chance.

"I will be keeping close track of events as they transpire," Wong told the Dragon.

"I assumed no less," his comrade said, the silky tone almost a physical caress. "Keep me advised."

"Of course."

The line dead, a hollow sound in Wong's ear until he cradled the receiver. There was much to do, despite his distance from the fighting yet to come.

And he couldn't afford to fail.

16

The Golden Triangle

The jungle east of Mandalay, along the Salween River, was a steaming no-man's land. Two hours and forty minutes from Rangoon, the landing strip came out of nowhere, hacked from living jungle by the only means available—which meant machetes, axs, fire and sweat. A month from now, if no one came around to keep the land clear, it would be reclaimed by Mother Nature with a vengeance, but the four men who were dropped there, moments short of dusk, cared nothing for the distant future. They were focused absolutely on the here and now.

With Sein Salong to guide them, Bolan and his Phoenix Force allies reckoned they would have a decent chance of finding Tuan Khoo's stronghold in the Golden Triangle. Surviving once they got there was a different proposition altogether, and they still had some misgivings—most of them expressed by Yakov Katzenelenbogen—that the Burmese guide might lead them into a trap. In that event, they were agreed, Salong would be among the first to die, but they would trust him—cautiously—until he proved himself a traitor.

They spent an hour hiking eastward, then pitched camp when it became too dark to see the trail in front of them or distinguish twisted roots from cobras stretched across the path. They camped without a fire, ate candy bars and cold

beans, washed down with water from their own canteens. Their breakfast was identical, and they were on the trail again by dawn, determined to lose no more time than absolutely necessary.

Tuan Khoo controlled a territory half the size of Delaware. His word was law within that jungle kingdom, where he held the undisputed power of life and death. His serfs included some three thousand Chinese soldiers, many of them second-generation warriors in the drug trade, plus an equal number of Chinese, Burmese and Thai camp followers—the women, children and civilian lackeys who provided Khoo's army with supplies and services that ranged from food and sex to hand-washed clothes and the repair of their machines. Beyond Khoo's base camp, several dozen villages survived by cultivating poppies, harvesting raw opium and selling it to Khoo at a fraction of the price he would receive once it was processed, packaged and exported to the outside world.

And life went on... for some.

By half past noon on Sunday, Bolan's penetration team was well inside the territory ruled by Khoo. Their pace had slowed dramatically, as they were forced to watch for booby traps along the way, as well as Chinese sentries and patrols. Nor could they trust the local Burmese villagers, whose livelihood depended on the drug trade, even as their very lives depended on a show of loyalty to the warlord. Anyone they met from that point on might try to kill them, or at least betray them to the nearest squad of riflemen from Khoo's camp.

And since they were depending on surprise for any hope they had of getting out alive, a premature alarm would spell disaster.

That they reached the warlord's stronghold without tripping any signal flares or rousing hostile villagers was due in equal parts to Salong's methodical approach to stalking and the combat expertise of those he led. Four soldiers, one of

them an almost total stranger to the other three, had forged themselves into a war machine that would be lethal to the enemy, despite its tiny size.

Three thousand guns to four—perhaps as many as five thousand, if a fair percentage of the hangers-on were armed. It had to be the worst odds Bolan had encountered since he launched his one-man war against the Mafia so long ago, but the statistics only told a partial story. Once you factored in the human elements of courage, dedication, training and sheer audacity, the odds began to change. Still grim, but Bolan knew that anything could happen once the dice were tossed and they began to play for keeps.

The camp was huge, a town carved from the jungle, larger than some hamlets back in the American Midwest. Four men could lose themselves in there... unless three of them happened to be round-eyes wearing camouflage fatigues and packing arms enough to stop a full battalion in its tracks.

"This is the place," Salong informed him with a crooked smile. "I got you here, as promised. Now the rest is up to you."

"We'll wait for dark to make our move," Bolan said. "In the meantime I suggest we have a look around."

THE BURMESE JUNGLE WAS a living hell for Chik Fu. Despite their elevation in the mountains, it was scorching hot by day, with that same ninety-five percent humidity that air-conditioning helped him endure back in Rangoon. The closest thing to air-conditioning in Tuan Khoo's camp were the electric fans that operated from a central generator, stirring muggy air with no real vestige of relief from the oppressive heat. Sundown reduced the temperature a bit, to somewhere in the eighties, but it also brought out the biting, stinging insects in force to feast on human sweat and blood.

Fu sat in his tent, surrounded by mosquito netting, with his feet immersed in tepid water, cursing Edward Wong for

the enlightened plan that put him there, among barbarians, where every passing hour was like a week in Hell. Back in the city, even if his enemies were stalking him, at least Fu could have waited for them in the comfort of his air-conditioned penthouse, sipping vintage wine and listening to CDs on his stereo, perhaps with a young lady to help distract him while he waited for the end.

To live like this, though, when he wasn't even hiding, rather waiting—hoping—for the enemy to find him so that Khoo could corner them and shoot them down like animals...it made no sense at all. If he went through all this for nothing, and the round-eyes killed him anyway—

Fu's stomach growled, reminding him that he couldn't eat when he wanted to, but had to wait for mess call, a description that was wholly accurate in its assessment of the culinary fare available in camp. It was amazing that an army could survive on fruit, rice and stringy beef for years on end, but Fu saw no reason why he ought to share their voluntary sacrifice.

It was a form of punishment, he told himself, for letting things get out of hand around Rangoon—as if he had a choice, the round-eyes coming in from Europe after ravaging their allies there with absolute impunity. It wasn't *his* fault that this plague had fallen on the 14K, but Wong had chosen him as an example to the other red poles—those who still survived. Fu would be staked out like a goat to draw the tiger into range, and if the plan failed...well, he would remember these days in the jungle next time anything went wrong on his home turf, perhaps respond more forcefully next time to nip a problem in the bud.

It could be worse, of course. Wong could have simply had him killed. Such fates were not unknown for red poles who had fallen out of favor in the hill chief's eyes.

The first shot seemed to echo from the far side of the camp. Off somewhere to the west, but Fu couldn't be sure. Sounds were deceptive in the jungle, more so in the moun-

tains, and it wouldn't be uncommon for a gun to be discharged around a military base.

And yet...

In seconds flat he heard more firing. Automatic weapons opened up on the perimeter, sent brilliant tracers arcing through the night. The shock of an explosion rocked the camp, immediately followed by another—and the lights went out.

Fu knocked his bucket over as he scrambled from his chair. He got tangled up in the mosquito netting for a moment, ripping through it with his bare hands, moving toward the simple cot and nightstand where his boots and pistol waited for him.

It was time. The enemy had found him.

But the tethered goat wasn't about to put his trust in strangers, much less sit and wait until the tiger swallowed him alive.

THE FIRST SHOT BROUGHT McCarter to his feet. He couldn't tell if it was Bolan's weapon or a Chinese sentry's, and it made no difference to the plan. Once *anybody* started shooting, they had orders to advance, seek out the targets they had drawn by lots that afternoon and set about the job of wreaking havoc in the camp. Survival was considered a priority, but they were here to kick some ass, with some specific targets on the hit list, and McCarter hadn't traveled all this way to turn around and go home empty-handed.

Not when he could teach his enemies a thing or two about the taste and smell of primal fear.

McCarter came in from the darkness, dressed from head to toe in jungle camouflage, his tanned face covered by a commando head net, carrying a Chinese knock off of the famous AK-47. His position on the south side of the camp gave him a fair shot at the motor pool and mess tent, but his first priority was knocking out the generator hut and cutting power to the camp.

A roving sentry saw him coming and opened his mouth to shout a warning, but McCarter got there first. His rifle butt caved in the sentry's teeth and slammed his jaw back several inches, cutting off the shout that would have summoned reinforcements. He delivered one more stroke when the sentry was down to keep him there, a limp form in the moonlight.

It was no trick picking out the generator shed, with cables radiating outward like the tentacles of an anemic squid, its diesel engine puttering away to keep the juice on for the camp. McCarter made it all the way without another incident, but there was steady firing on the fringes of the camp by now. His comrades were catching hell, and he wouldn't pass through the ranks so easily if he was headed in the opposite direction.

No one had thought of locking up the generator shed. McCarter stepped inside, switched on a naked bulb that dangled overhead and took a block of plastique from the satchel slung across his shoulder. He set the detonator with a short fuse, counting down from twenty at a click per second, and was back outside in no time.

It went to hell from there.

The Chinese soldier nearly stumbled over him, blinked twice and then let out a whooping war cry as he recognized a hostile stranger in the camp. His rifle was a carbon copy of McCarter's, but he couldn't match the former SAS commando's personal reaction time. Before the khaki soldier had a chance to bring up his weapon, McCarter kicked him in the groin, stepped back and slammed a 3-round burst into his chest.

How much time was left before the generator blew? Instead of pondering the question, he was on his way, a flitting shadow, jostling soldiers and civilians as he ran, his rifle spitting death when two young sentries moved to block his path.

He had to have covered twenty yards before the shock wave of the blast reached out and lifted him off his feet, tossed him head over heels and dropped him sprawling on his back. McCarter barely kept his weapon, but his lungs gave up their air. Colored specks of light danced on the inside of his eyelids as he fought to keep his grip on consciousness.

Hang on, a small voice cautioned him.

He struggled to his hands and knees, then somehow made it to his feet, head swimming, feeling as if he should vomit.

No time for that, he told himself. The choices were to fight or die, with no safe ground between the two extremes.

McCarter made his choice and came out fighting, wondering if it would be enough to save his life.

TUAN KHOO WAS the self-appointed general of an army recognized by no one but himself. He wasn't old enough, at fifty-three, to have seen military service under Chiang Kai-shek before the Communists devoured his native China, but he had grown up in exile with the men who fought those battles and were forced at last to run away. If anything, Khoo's anticommunism was more radical than theirs, because he knew the enemy by reputation only and was willing to believe sometimes exaggerated stories, never doubting for a moment that their evil was immense and all-consuming.

At the same time, though, the general had a private empire to protect. His lifelong war to "liberate" Red China had become primarily a war of words, with rare border raids to make his soldiers think that they were fighting for some cause beyond the daily price of opium. In truth, if General Khoo was forced to choose between remaining in the Golden Triangle, where he made all the rules, and going "home" to live in an ideal Chinese democracy, he would have stayed precisely where he was.

And now the empire he had carved out for himself was being threatened. Only marginally, it was true—the way a scorpion may threaten a bull elephant—but even one sting from a scorpion, if left untreated, could cause disability and death.

Khoo left his quarters in full uniform, proceeding toward the sound of gunfire on the camp's perimeter. That was to say, he chose a compass point at random, since the whole perimeter was firing now, and moved in *that* direction arbitrarily. He had to start somewhere, try to find out what his men were shooting at and whether there was anything at all to challenge them outside the camp.

That question was answered for him well before he reached the western border of the camp. A loud explosion echoed through the sprawling compound, and the camp went dark. It didn't take a genius to work out that someone had deliberately destroyed the generator with an explosive charge.

Which meant that there were enemies inside the camp.

Khoo hesitated, thought of turning back to find Chik Fu and shake him until his eyeteeth rattled, find out what he *really* had in mind when he and Edward Wong devised their "master plan" to place an enemy of unknown strength on Tuan Khoo's very doorstep. Idiots!

And he had been a fool to play along.

It was too late for self-recriminations, though. Khoo had to bring the situation under his control and swiftly now, before his men lost every semblance of the discipline he had been pounding into them for years. They drilled regularly, of course, and most of them were fairly decent shots, but they had never really fought a battle in their lives. The village raids and scouting parties certainly didn't prepare them for the kind of action that was coming to them now.

They weren't seasoned men of war.

And neither, come to think of it, was General Tuan Khoo.

But he could fake it with the best of them, and he wasn't about to let his men see any sign of weakness in his own demeanor. He would die before revealing anything that smacked of indecision to his soldiers. They depended on him to be strong, and Khoo depended on himself.

It seemed impossible that all his men, on every side of the encampment, could be sighting down on flesh-and-blood enemies. Someone had started shooting, and now the rest of them were dueling shadows in the forest, killing trees and bushes, maybe here and there a rodent or a jungle cat.

And yet there *was* an enemy. Someone had blown the generator hut and left the camp in darkness. Running figures jostled Khoo as he stood with a couple of his aides, uncertain now where he should go. The only place in camp where he was certain of a hostile presence was behind him, toward the burned-out generator shed.

"This way!"

Khoo turned on his heel and doubled back in the direction he had come from. His aides kept up with difficulty, roughly shoving anyone who blocked their path. Khoo had no reason to believe that he would find the bomber lingering around the site, admiring his own handiwork, but it was still a starting point.

And anything was possible.

In fact, he almost failed to recognize the man who stepped in front of him, some fifty feet or so from the shattered generator. That wasn't to say he knew the man, per se, but rather knew, upon a second glance, that he was out of place. He was too tall for one thing, and his uniform was wrong. The pale moonlight showed tiger-striped fatigues, when khaki was the normal uniform. And what was there about his face? It was a kind of blur, as if—

Khoo snapped up his rifle, was thumbing off the safety, when his enemy unleashed a long burst from the hip. General Khoo staggered as the bullets ripped into his abdomen, below the rib cage. Squeezing off a short burst of his own,

he knew that it was wasted as he toppled over backward and fell across the legs of someone stretched out on the ground.

One of his aides?

He couldn't tell and didn't care.

Khoo tried to rise but couldn't force his legs to follow the commands that issued from his brain. Too late he felt the shadow fall across his upturned face and saw the figure of his enemy blot out the stars.

"Na shi shen-me yi-si?"

But General Khoo already knew exactly what it meant, and he didn't expect an answer as the man-shape turned away from him, with no reply.

It meant the end.

KATZ DROPPED THE FIRST two Chinese soldiers with a single burst, then swung around to face their comrade, ducking as the gunner opened fire from forty feet away. It was a close thing, with Katzenelenbogen squeezing off another burst before he was prepared, dumbfounded when it cut the soldier's legs from under him and brought him down.

Not dead, but down.

The gunner tried to rise, but this time Katz was ready for him, squeezing off another burst that caught him in the chest and flipped him on his back.

All done.

The barracks buildings were immediately to his left, and Katz pushed off in that direction even as he struggled to his feet. The rifle hung across his chest, its sling biting into Katz's shoulder while he palmed a frag grenade and used his claw to yank the pin.

No time to hesitate now, not with the barracks right in front of him, a second shift of soldiers grappling with their clothes and weapons, trying to respond in timely fashion to the roaring chaos just outside their door.

He lobbed the first grenade through brittle glass, hurled a second through an open door and was already reaching for a third when the first one detonated, jagged shrapnel rattling on the inside of the corrugated metal Quonset hut. The second blast came close behind the first, and men were screaming in the barracks, though not as many as were shouting seconds earlier.

He left them to it, with another barracks just in front of him. Katz dropped his third grenade inside an open window and kept running, clutching the AK-47 with his good left hand as two young soldiers cleared the doorway just in front of him.

Half-dressed and still bleary-eyed from sleep, they scarcely recognized death coming for them in the night. Katz shot them both from less than fifteen feet away, the impact of his bullets spinning the gunners and slamming them to earth like rag dolls, dead before they hit the ground.

His third grenade exploded then, the shock wave buckling a portion of the hut's wall. Katz staggered, kept his footing and was ready with a fourth grenade before he reached a window at the far end of the smoky barracks. Someone's face was pressed against the glass as Katz made his pitch, but face and frag grenade both disappeared inside the hut, obliterated seconds later by a fiery thunderclap.

He still had four grenades left and another barracks coming up, when Sein Salong's machine gun started spraying tracers in the "wrong" direction, through the heart of Khoo's camp. That meant the plan was still on track, for what it might be worth. Four men against such overwhelming numbers that Katz didn't want to think about it anymore.

The plan wasn't to wipe them out, of course; that would have been impossible, unless they had been able to acquire a small nuclear missile from their contacts in Rangoon. Without that kind of punch, however, they would have to

pick and choose selected targets if they could, go for the hostile leadership as much as possible and count on chaos to assist them in withdrawing when their work was done.

The little two-way radio on Katzenelenbogen's belt erupted into static as he primed the fifth grenade. He hesitated, keeping to the shadows, waiting for a message. Would it be a voice he recognized, or had the enemy killed one of his companions? Were they toying with the radio to see what they could learn of the attacking force?

"Scratch General Khoo," McCarter said to anyone with ears on, and the radio went silent once again.

Katz smiled and left the shadows, closing on the third hut where soldiers had been sleeping before their enemies had found them. He lobbed the frag grenade through a window and gripped his rifle, waiting for the blast before he kicked the door in and charged across the threshold. Muzzle-flashes lit the startled faces, some of them already smeared with soot and blood. They couldn't understand a word he said, but it was all the same to Katz. The blood was singing in his ears, and he was shouting at his nameless adversaries.

"Rise and shine, you bastards! Rise and shine!"

IT WAS NEITHER FLUKE nor fate that led the Executioner to Chik Fu. He had the red pole spotted within twenty minutes of beginning his surveillance on the jungle camp. Fu occupied a tent not far from General Khoo's, the leaders close enough to keep in touch without invading one another's private space.

He knew where he was going when the lights went out, determined not to blow it in the darkness and confusion of a fight on unfamiliar ground. The superficial details of the camp were filed away in Bolan's memory, but there was nothing he could do about the soldiers or civilians who were bound to run amok once shooting started and the generator blew.

Too bad.

He had his fix, his mission, and unless a bullet brought him down, he wouldn't deviate from his appointed course. When he encountered soldiers on the way, or armed civilians, Bolan dealt with them and kept on moving, leaving a trail of bodies in his wake that anyone could follow if the trackers weren't distracted by the task of fighting for their lives. It stood to reason that his target would be moving, too, and he could only keep his fingers crossed that Fu had been asleep or unprepared for trouble when the shooting started. A little break was all he needed.

He saw the tent in front of him, a faint glow from within that had to be a lamp or flashlight, since the generator was no longer feeding power to the camp. A shadow moved between the light and canvas, huge, distorted. As Bolan moved closer to the tent, the light went out.

The radio attached to Bolan's combat harness sputtered into life and he heard McCarter's voice: "Scratch General Khoo."

The Executioner rushed the tent in time to see a slender silhouette emerging from the open flap in front. Just then, a swarm of tracers passed between them, making Bolan blink, and two or three burned through the fabric of the tent. Flames caught and held, their light revealing Bolan's target as he raised a pistol, sighting down the slide.

Fu's first shot would have done the job if Bolan hadn't thrown himself aside. His jarring impact with the earth made the warrior hesitate, a brief delay, but still enough for Fu to try a second shot. The bullet traced a line of fire across one thigh, but not deep enough to reach the bone. Bolan came up firing with his Chinese rifle, holding down the trigger, stitching Fu from crotch to throat and blowing him away.

Bolan's leg protested as he scrambled to his feet, but pain would have to wait. He started falling back toward the perimeter and palmed the little two-way radio, his thumb on the transmitter switch.

"Scratch Fu," he stated. "That's a wrap. We're out of here. Confirm!"

McCarter's voice was first to answer: "That's affirmative. I'm pulling out."

"Suits me," Katz added. "I'll see you soon."

And silence from the final member of their team.

He tried again. "Salong! Confirm instructions!"

There was no response, and only silence from the dark stretch of perimeter where Sein Salong had manned a captured .50-caliber submachine gun short moments earlier.

Goddammit!

Bolan turned his back on regret and jogged toward the jungle, dodging adversaries where he could, eliminating two or three who crossed his path by sheer bad luck.

The job was done, but it had cost them dearly. Bolan was determined that his newfound friend wouldn't have died in vain. Beyond the Burmese mountains, farther east, more enemies were waiting for him, still believing they were safe.

The Executioner was on his way to show them they were wrong.

* * * * *

Don't miss the exciting conclusion of
THE RED DRAGON *trilogy.*
Look for The Executioner #212,
RIDE THE BEAST, in August.